Dedicated affectionately
to the anxious, the worried, the stressed,
and the generally freaked out

1

FINAL PREPARATIONS

Okay. Let's start this awful, one-for-the-books day at the beginning. That's where most stories start, I guess.

I'm looking in the bathroom mirror, and what I see is decent. A bit gangly and skinny, but not terrible. Inside, I have the regular stew of butterflies and worries and some irritation that a certain someone's nasty, yellowed nighttime mouthguard was leaning on the bristles of my toothbrush this morning—but I take a couple of deep breaths. I actually feel halfway all right about what the mirror is showing me for once.

I clean up okay, as every adult likes to say when a kid puts in the slightest effort.

I wash my hands one more time—I'd used a tissue to move the mouthguard, but who knows if that's at all effective. Gross stuff can probably pass through a tissue like air through a screen door.

I walk out into the kitchen, and my mom is there, waiting excitedly.

"Oh. You look absolutely perfect."

She says that, but then she must see something wrong, because she does that disgusting mom move where she licks her thumb and wipes at something beside my mouth. A stray bit of scrambled egg? A toast crumb?

"Gross."

AUTHOR'S NOTE:
IT'S MORE THAN GROSS.
I HATE GERMS.
IT'S A THING.

As I wipe any residual spit away, she sits back, grabs my shoulders, and holds me at arm's length.

"Look at this. Yes sir. That's my handsome man." Her eyes dart around from my new shirt to my fresh—one day old!—haircut. She smiles.

I haven't seen much of that smile lately. I've seen a lot more of the stressed side-frown. The Susan Yaeger Chewing-Her-Lip Worry Face—which typically gives me the Andrew Yaeger Worried Stomach.

She pats my shoulders twice. "Mika and Jonesy'll be here any minute, and I need to get to my Big First Day." Today is her first day as executive assistant to some big important business guy, and we're both stomach-churningly aware of how much she needs it to go well.

My grandmother, G, shuffles into the room in her neon-pink housecoat. She's been living with us for the past year and a half or so. She stops in the middle of the kitchen and looks around, confused. Her graying hair looks like she got in a fight with her pillows.

My mom turns on her caregiver smile. "Hi, Mom. Can

I get you anything?" She pulls a few cinnamon graham crackers—G's favorite—out of the cupboard. G takes them, scratches her butt, and stands there staring at me like she's not quite sure who I am.

"Doesn't Andrew look nice, Mom? You always said looking nice for school photos was super important. It's Picture Day!"

At the words *Picture Day,* my grandmother's face lights up a bit—like the old G I used to know. She holds up a finger and croaks a quiet "Oh, yes, yes, yes." Then she hurries (as much as she can) out of the room.

That's the most excitement we've seen from G in weeks. "You can't take the teacher out of the lady," my mom says. "She used to get so worked up over school photos. Said 'Those photos are how people will remember you forever.' She wasn't completely wrong, either. Somebody I went to school with friend-requested me the other day. I had no idea who she was until I got out my yearbook, and BOOM. Her school photo brought it all back."

G walks back into the room—her arms full of middle school yearbooks. They're from *my* school, but they're ancient.

G used to teach Social Studies at my school. Waaaay back. She taught there for years. I can't count the number of times we've been stopped by former students at restaurants, thanking her and telling me what a great teacher she was. It's kind of cool, I guess—although sometimes you just want to eat your mac and cheese bites in peace, y'know? It's like living with a minor celebrity.

G thumps the books down. The stack spills over a bit, but she grabs the top one and opens it with a shaky hand. A number of individual photos—the kind you buy to give to friends—tumble out. Maybe fifteen of them. All students. I look up and G has a huge, proud grin on her face as she pages through to the faculty page. When she finds it, she spins the book around and points at her black-and-white photo. It's a great picture—she's a lot younger, her hair is darker, and she's wearing some kind of a vest that looks like it came out of an ancient sitcom.

Mrs. Hanley - Social Studies

"Pretty good, huh?" I look up and she's waggling her eyebrows. "Huh?" It's so good to see her happy that my mom and I both laugh. She nods and grabs another yearbook. While she's looking, I pick up a few of the student photos. They all have writing on them:

For Mrs. Hanley—You are the best! Kaitlyn

Thank you so much Mrs. Hanley! Marcus

Have a great summer, Mrs. H! Jennifer

I can't thank you enough.—Bob

Seems like they liked her a lot, which doesn't surprise me. She was super fun and cool—before she started getting sick.

She shows me a couple more of her photos, where

she's wearing different but similar vests. Vests must have been her official yearbook photo look. Then she puts her hand on my shoulder and gives it a faint squeeze.

"You look good." She smiles, but then straightens her back and pats her chest, looking me in the eye. "Up straight." Then she pulls a second graham cracker out of her nightgown pocket and takes a bite. (The woman would eat them all day long if my mom didn't keep them out of sight.) She looks down at the pile of yearbooks and back up at me, then turns around and starts shuffling back to her (my old) room. As she goes through the doorway, she lets out a fairly impressive burp.

Unfortunately, G isn't "all there" these days.

I grab my backpack. I packed it last night—perfectly, as always. Everything in its proper compartment. (I have a system.) I put both straps over my shoulders, careful not to wrinkle the new shirt. I can't remember the last time I had a Brand-New Shirt. One that isn't a hand-me-down from my weird cousin in Des Moines. And this sucker has a collar, no less!

"Wait. Wait. Let me get a picture." My mom grabs her iPhone—maybe the oldest iPhone still in circulation—and waves her hand for me to get over in front of the plants.

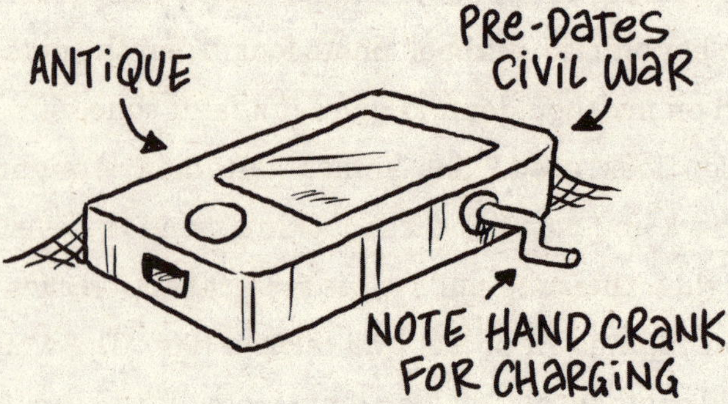

I watch her struggling to get the camera app to come up.

"You sure you don't want me to skip today?" I ask. "I could ride along. Give moral support. Maybe a pep talk over lunch?"

"No way, pal. I'm riding solo today and YOU are gonna go get the best school picture of your life. Your sixth-grade photo looked like you were kidnapped or raised by wolves or something. But not this year, my well-put-together friend."

She's nervous. Which makes me nervous. She needs this job to work out. It could change things—and we really need things to change. And yep, as she aims the phone she's chewing at that lip again—right on schedule. I feel something in my stomach twist. It's nerves. Anxiety. But it feels like there's a fussy iguana in there.

THE ANXIETY FILES A. YAEGER
ANXIETY 101
GOT A FUSSY IGUANA IN YOUR STOMACH?
BOY, DO I!
GRR
HEY! ANXIETY!
FEEL NERVOUS ELECTRICITY IN YER SHOULDERS?
YUP!
YEP! THAT'S IT!
SWARM OF CAFFEINATED EELS IN YOUR HEAD?
SSS
CHECK!
SSS
SSS
NOW YOU'RE GETTING IT!
WANT TO LEAVE YOUR BRAIN SOMEWHERE AND GO HIDE?
AND HOW!
THAT'S THE STUFF!

"Okay, Chin up. Up straight. Big smile. Million dollars!"

I do it as best I can, but I'm in my head.

"Good luck, Mom. I know you're gonna slay." She's been playing that song where Beyoncé sings about slaying on a loop for a couple of days. Psyching herself up.

She sips her coffee. "Thank you. I *intend* to slay. But don't worry about me, okay? I mean it. Just focus on having a good day and try not to mess up that shirt or your hair or whatever. I won't be available to bring you a replacement, so don't spill anything on it. What period are you getting your photos?"

"No idea."

"Well, I hope it's early." She stares at me, but I can

tell she's not actually looking at me. She's thinking. She darts off and comes back with my nicest T-shirt—the blue one—and hands it to me. "Put this in your backpack. Just in case. I really do want your photo to be nice this year. For you, but also for me. And for G! Oh, and I put some of those stain remover packet things in with your lunch."

I slide the shirt into the back pocket by my ancient school-provided laptop. It irritates me, as I had everything just how I like it, but I don't say anything. Adding the shirt bunches up my sack lunch, and I just know my PB&J is going to come out looking like smushed-up bread origami.

I put the pack on again and it doesn't feel right. I'm a weirdo when it comes to my backpack, I'm aware. I tap the kitchen table five times without thinking about it. I fight the overwhelming urge to take everything out and repack it. Well, more than an urge, it's a little voice telling me I need to. Or something might . . . happen. But there's no time, and I don't want to make my mom more nervous. Maybe I can repack on the bus. Not fixing it makes my chest feel tight.

There's a knock on the apartment door as it swings open. "Hallooooo?" It's my best friend, Jonesy, and her mom, Mika (my mom's best friend). They step in as my mom shushes Jonesy.

"Shh shh shh. I'm hoping she's going back to sleep." Meaning G. Mika has a stack of *Peoples* and *Us Weeklys* under her arm. She's going to watch G for the day while my mom goes to work. (I should have said: My grandma has Alzheimer's disease and it's gotten pretty bad, pretty fast—some days she forgets who we are or why she lives here. And she kind of likes to wander. That's part of why my mom needs this new big job—so we can get her more help.)

"Whoa. Who's this fancy person, and what have you done with my friend Andrew?" Jonesy gives me a dramatic look up and down. "Combed hair? Ironed shorts? Nice!"

I roll my eyes. Normally I'd meet Jonesy on the bus after she catches it in her (much nicer) neighborhood, but today Mika brought her, so she gets to hang with me at my bus stop. Speaking of which, we need to hustle if we don't want to miss it.

I give my mom a bear hug. "Okay. We gotta go. Good luck today. Be awesome. Break a leg."

She laughs. "No, YOU break a leg! Be awesome! Love you!"

"Love you." I kind of mumble it as I turn—all too aware of Jonesy. I mean, I love my mom, but in front of other people it's just kind of weird saying it. I give Jonesy another little eye roll as I pass her, just to keep my street cred.

Then Jonesy and I are in the hallway. It smells like Mrs. Partridge is cooking broccoli in 3G—again—and I'm a little embarrassed for Jonesy to smell it. So gross. Who cooks broccoli at this time of the morning? Old people, I guess. Or maybe they make broccoli Pop-Tarts for older people?

We fly down the stairs. As we go by, Mr. Benchley is in the vestibule. He looks up over his glasses, perched on the very tip of his nose. (I swear he must glue them there.)

"Holy cow! Looking good, Andrew! What's the special occasion?"

I look back as I push through the glass front door. "Picture Day. Gotta look our best, y'know?" I shrug and we head out.

1.5

Hold on.

I feel like I brushed over the whole "my grandma has Alzheimer's" thing—and it's something I need to go into. Because it's pretty awful.

So, this is Chapter 1.5, okay. My book, my rules.

G—I've always called her G 'cause she liked that "better than Grandma or Grammy or Gee Goo"—has been a gigantic part of my life for as long as I can remember, and lately she's just sort of . . . fading away.

I mean, she's still there, right in front of us, but a lot of the things that made her who she was are drifting away. Like, her love of whacked-out, experimental baking. Or the way she used to gesture with her hands when she talked—something I inherited from her. Or how she'd make her famous Movie Theater Popcorn. She knew how to make it taste just like the stuff you'd get in a theater—better, even—and she'd get those red-and-white-striped tubs they have there to make it feel even more authentic. Comfy clothes, a blanket, her popcorn, and a movie or a game of Scrabble were the recipe for a great night at her condo.

But there's also the way she was always so into what was going on in the world. She's always been a superfan of news of all kinds. Local, national, international, political, money stuff.

She used to teach middle school social studies way

back when, and she said going through the paper each day with her students was always part of her class. As long as my mom can remember, she'd read the paper first thing every day and watch the local *and* national news every night, plus more where she could find it. She read three different news magazines, cover to cover. But now she's just . . . not interested anymore. In much of anything. It's so not like her. She mostly looks out the window a lot now.

Maybe the thing that I miss the most is her laugh. She had one of the best laughs in the world. It was loud, abrupt, and it would burst out of her like nothing on earth was gonna stop it. My mom called it a blurt laugh, and it was, but then it would go on for a while. She'd laugh until tears came out of her eyes and we all worried she couldn't breathe. My mom and I still play Scrabble from time to time, but without that laugh shaking the thin apartment walls, it doesn't feel the same. It sucks—pardon my French.

G was always a little bit of a space cadet. She'd tell you that herself.

But a few years ago, things started getting worse. G started really having trouble remembering words.

I remember one particular day we were playing Scrabble at her condo's kitchen table while she was baking some new weird cookies. (She experimented with cookie recipes like a mad scientist, and they didn't always work out. Some were great, but some . . . Wow. Remind me to tell you about the Catastrophic Honey Mustard Cookie Mess of Death sometime.)

"Are you gonna stare at your tiles all day or are you gonna play, genius?" G talked to me like an adult, which is another thing I've always loved about her.

"Hold your horses, lady." I made a face without looking up.

She sipped her tea while I tried to make my letters assemble into a word. Any word. I was wondering if SQUIX might be something when the oven beeped. She hopped up, pulling on her well-used oven mitts. When she opened the oven door, the smell was amazing. She pulled the cookies out and took them over to the sink for an Official G Inspection. She sniffed them, wafting the smell toward her nose with a mitt. Then she got down to eye level with them and poked lightly at two or three.

"Andrew. Hand me the . . . um . . ." She didn't finish. She looked over at me, still crouched over. "The . . . thing."

"What thing?" I smiled and tipped my head to the side. Giving her a hard time.

She laughed but closed her eyes. "Oh, for cryin' out . . . The flat thing." She stood up, giving me a disgusted look. "This thing." She waved her flat hand around. Acted out sliding it under the cookies.

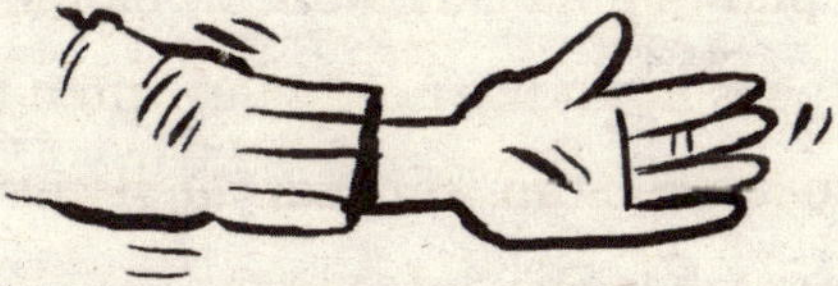

She walked to the pot by the stove where she kept the utensils. She grabbed her metal spatula and waved it at me. "This, ya ding-dong. You know what I needed."

Then she just stood there, looking at the spatula in her hand for a while. She chuckled and looked at me. "Why can I not come up with the name for this?"

I laughed, but then watched her smile fade a little. Her eyebrow twitched down for just a second. Then she looked up at me.

I wasn't sure she wanted me to tell her, but it came out. "Spatula?"

"SPATULA!" Her arms shot into the air. "Good lord! I went completely blank! It was like my brain turned to pudding for a minute there. Thank you."

It's funny. As she got worse, that image of her brain turning to pudding quickly went from amusing to disturbing. It pops up in my head more often than I'd like. But she said it, and I can still hear the slight laugh in her raspy G voice when she did.

So, maybe that was the beginning of the serious stuff.

Or maybe it wasn't. Maybe it was just a common everyday brain fart. Either way, things started getting worse. It was six or seven months later when she couldn't quite think of my name one day. A few months after that she forgot my mom's name at a block party. Her own daughter. I mean, she only forgot for a few seconds—but it wasn't long before it was a common thing. And then one day she seemed completely confused about who I was.

It was the scariest thing I'd ever experienced. Besides my mom, she probably knew me better than anyone in the world, and then . . . all that love and trust and knowledge. Just, gone. How could that be? It was gut-wrenching.

That's when things started to get really bad. There was an incident where instead of coming home from her hair appointment, she just randomly drove up to Indianapolis. She called my mom and had no idea how to get home or where she was.

Not long after that she had to move in with us, and I let her have my room because of course that's what you do, but it means I have to sleep on the stupid fold-out couch in the front room with the sun coming through the blinds at the crack of dawn and I have to keep my clothes in the coat closet and she's super messy and sometimes she stays in the bathroom for forever and we don't know if she's actually doing something or she's zombie'd out and just staring off . . . and I really miss my room and my stuff and my space and . . .

Sorry.

I love G, but . . .

Wow.

I guess I needed to get that out.

2

JONESY

Jones, Aisha

Jonesy and I climb onto the bus and grab our usual second-row seat—with her by the window the way she likes. It's the perfect seat, in that we have easy on and off, but we're not in the front row, where Darren the bus driver always tries to talk with us about *Stranger Things.* (He tries to talk to everyone about *Stranger Things.* The man is obsessed.) Jonesy is usually able to secure this seat because her neighborhood is an earlier stop, but today it's still available. I guess people just think of it as our seat at this point.

Jonesy takes off her backpack and gives my new shirt another look as I start rearranging things inside my pack. (It loosens my chest and shuts up that little voice inside me.)

"So, what's with the proper young gentleman look? That's a new shirt, right?"

"It is. Snazzy, huh?" She's wearing her same old Pacers jersey—it's her favorite and she wears it all the time. "You do know it's Picture Day, right?"

"Yeah, so?" She smiles and shrugs.

Jonesy has been my best friend since before I could chew solid food. Seriously. We were basically matched up at birth. Our moms were college roommates at IU, and then they each got married about the same time and then they had us about the same time and we've barely spent any time apart since we entered the world. But we both agree that we would have made our way to being friends even if that wasn't the case. Sometimes, things are just meant to be.

That said, we're different. Quite a bit different. I mean, for starters, she's a girl and I'm a guy. I'm annoyingly tall and she's tiny. She's a natural athlete and I'm . . . not a natural athlete. She's obsessed with sea life and watches YouTube videos about them all the time and Shark Week is better than Christmas for her. Her parents actually "adopted" a shark named Kamo for her for her birthday last year—she has a certificate and a photo of it in her room. I'm more into . . . comics and movies. I'm a germ-obsessed neat freak and she probably has a gummy bear stuck to her somewhere at this very moment. And finally, she's Black while I'm about as pasty White as they come. But somehow, we just fit. The best of best friends.

Her actual name is Aisha Jones, but she insists everyone just call her Jones or Jonesy.

She's feeling the sleeve of my shirt. "This is nice. Soft. Did you get it just for your picture?"

"Yep. Mom splurged. Got me a haircut at an actual salon too." Jones knows that my mom usually cuts my hair over a towel in our kitchen. I turn my head sideways, posing.

"Oh, yeah! I thought it looked better! No Flowbee?"

"Nope. The lady who washed my hair gave me a scalp massage and everything. I'm like a new—"

Just then I get slammed—hard—in the side of the face and shoulder by a giant, overstuffed backpack. It feels like it's packed full of rocks. Rubbing my cheek, I turn around to see Gene Phillips glaring at me.

Gene Phillips is one to avoid. He's not a big guy, but he's four feet eight inches of Mean. He's all skinny, tough muscle. Like he's made entirely out of gristle. He also for some reason wears sweat bands on his wrists like he's a '70s basketball player or something. I don't think it's a fashion choice. I think it's so he has something to push up his arms before he punches somebody in the face. He's well known for his face-punching.

Gene is also an interesting breed. The Incredibly Wealthy Bully. His dad is loaded—he owns a huge construction company. Phillips Construction. Their house has pillars, for cryin' out loud. I've seen it. I actually got invited to his birthday party in third grade—so I guess he wasn't always completely horrible. That party was wild. It was catered! And they had people dressed as Marvel characters! I still have a photo of me with Iron Man up in my room that was taken there. I've never been back, but it was the nicest house I've ever been in.

That said, all the pillars and Beats headphones and Vineyard Vines clothes in the world can't hide the mean.

"You got a problem, Yaeger?"

"Nope." I rub my cheek and straighten my glasses. "Ha ha. Sorry about that."

"Mow any good lawns, lately?" It's a dig at my after-school job. He stares.

"Nope. Just . . . just the usual."

After a few more uncomfortable moments, Gene keeps going down the aisle. I watch his brand-new name-brand backpack move away before looking down at my own. Faded, generic, fraying in a bunch of spots.

When I look up, Joncsy is staring at me.

"You just apologized to him for HIM smashing into YOUR head."

"I know. I know." I straighten my shirt. I feel the blood going to my cheeks. A hint of the familiar tightness in my chest. "It's just easier."

And safer. The only good interaction with Gene Phillips is a short one, I figure. He's seriously awful. "Is my hair all messed up?"

Jonesy shakes her head. "Your hair is fine. It's the rest of you I'm worried about."

I'm not entirely sure how to take that, so we ride in silence for a couple blocks as I fiddle with my backpack's zipper pulls. I *may* tap the seat five times to ward off impending doom.

I mean, I don't think Jonesy wants me to go toe-to-toe with Gene the Mean, but I'm aware she wishes I'd stand up for myself sometimes.

I hear Gene kicking some kid out of their seat a few rows back. "Move it, Frecklehead."

For my sake, Jonesy shakes the moment off. "Is your mom excited about the new job today?"

My stomach does a flip as I nod. "I think so. Maybe more excited about the bump in pay than the guy she'll be working for. He's supposed to be really, really tough—to put it nicely." I sniff and look at the back of Darren's head for a while. "But if we're gonna get G in that memory care facility . . ."

Jonesy knows what a big deal it is. She's heard how much it costs. And what a royal pain in the butt it is having her in our tiny apartment. And in my room. It's made me a bit of a crab at times.

"Susan's gonna kick this job in the butt. 'Cause she's a rock star. I don't care how much of a pill this boss is—Susan can tame him."

Jonesy calls my mom Susan and my mom calls her Jonesy in return. Her family is like my second family—the big difference being that her parents are still together, unlike mine. Her parents both have awesome jobs—her dad is really high up at the university and her mom does high-end real estate or something complicated where she wears business suits and always looks important. And they live in a super-cool, nice house with a circular driveway and an in-ground sprinkler system in a cool neighborhood, while we live in the broccoli-scented Sunset Vista apartments.

I'm going to do my best not to think about my mom's Big New Job today. That may sound harsh, or like I don't care—but it's the opposite. I care so much, it makes my toes curl. I have simmer-y nerves on a normal day, but today my nerves are already sizzling pretty good and we haven't even gotten to school yet.

Best to try to put it out of my mind.

I kind of have an issue with worrying. Stressing. Obsessing. Whatever you want to call it. Like sometimes I can lock up or spin out over a simple English assignment, or something stupid. One time, a few years ago, I just about came unglued in an arcade when I couldn't get a pair of SpongeBob sunglasses in one of those claw games. Not real proud of that.

I also have the tapping thing. I have a few tics—I guess that's what you'd call them. Like, tapping things five times. And I absolutely have to hit the pad of the finger only. If any fingernail touches the surface I'm tapping—or I think it might have—I start the five taps over or . . . I don't know what. I just do it.

Sometimes, I have to turn the light on and off five times, or until it feels right. And I check and recheck that the door is locked. I'll be all the way down the block and have to go back and all the way upstairs to double-check the apartment door. It's super annoying, but it feels like I don't have a choice. Or I'll have to shut my locker a few times until the *chunk* of closing it sounds just right. It feels like if I don't do it, something awful will happen. There's a little voice in my head that just won't shut up until I do it right. I know it makes no sense, but I can't get myself to stop. So, I just do it. It's easier than freaking out about it all day.

My mom even took me to a therapist a few times for this stuff—Dr. Cain—but I still do it. She explained it some and gave me some breathing exercises and a sketchbook to "draw my feelings" in and stuff that kinda sorta maybe helped? Results may vary.

Here's one of the first drawings I did. He's like my stand-in. I call him Tense Kid. He's kind of freaky-looking with his big eyes, but he sort of captures what I feel like at times:

I'll show some more of my sketches and cartoons—I call 'em the Anxiety Files—as we go. I'm no artist, but I have gotten better.

Anyway—back on the bus—I change the subject with Jonesy. Sometimes that's the best move. We don't want another SpongeBob eyewear situation on our hands. Or for me to start tapping all over the place.

"Don't you have a game tonight?" I ask. Despite her size, Jonesy's the best player on the seventh-grade girls' basketball team. By a lot.

"Yep. Ellettsville. They have a really good guard as well. Jennifer something. I think her dad played at Indiana State or somewhere."

"Yeah, well." I'm still adjusting my lunch, trying to un-smush it. "No match for the Jones-inator, I'm sure."

I know I'm the one who brought it up, but the basketball talk makes me antsy. Jonesy's been hanging out more and more with her teammates. I mean, I get it. I do. They all seem fine, and Jonesy always says I can hang with them too, but . . . Ugh. I know this'll sound like a little kid comment, but I liked it when it was just the two of us.

It makes me itchy when I think about it.

Danny Mitchell—he of the reddest hair in our school—turns around from the seat in front of us, sipping from a juice box. This kid loves juice.

I bob my head around in a "kind of" gesture. "I think so?" I get a small twinge of nerves, but I'm halfway decent in math, so it *should* be okay.

Jonesy is watching me as the bus slows down and humps over a speed bump. We're in the line of buses for the school's drop-off zone when she points. "You've got something on your shirt, Mr. Clean."

I pull at my sleeve and see a mark—maybe from Gene's backpack? Had he set it in something?

"Oh, you gotta be . . ." I reach into my lunch sack and pull out one of the little stain-wipe packets my mom dropped in there. Jonesy grabs it and tears it open.

"No Gene-stains today." She dabs and wipes at the spot. "Seems like this school photo means a lot to Susan, for some reason—so let's try to stay presentable, shall we?"

"Says the girl in the ancient, stained Reggie Miller jersey."

She grins. "Why mess with perfection?"

I pull my (carefully) folded hoodie from my backpack, which throws everything into disarray, but I figure I can repack it before first period, and it's worth it if it keeps my shirt clean. Messes and dirt and germs and gross stuff are everywhere—especially with middle school kids. I know that sounds weird coming from a fellow middle school kid, but what are you gonna do? Call me Neat Freak Yaeger.

I pull the hoodie on and feel just a tiny bit better, like I've donned a coat of armor to face the day.

The Anxiety Files
A.Y.
SOME OF THE WAYS ANXIETY FEELS
HEAVY HEAD
CRUSHING WEIGHT
1,000,000,
000,000,000
LBS
BEES
BZZ
BZZ
BZ
BZ
BZZ
BUZ
BZZZ
BZZ
BZZ
HOLE IN STOMACH

3

IN THE HALLS

Mitchell, Danny

A few minutes later, Jonesy and I are dodging our way through the front hallway of our school. She's venting a bit about her dad, who seems laser-focused on Jonesy playing in the WNBA, despite her height.

"He made me watch clips of Muggsy Bogues and Spud Webb last night. It's annoying."

I look back blankly, so she explains. "They were really

good, *short* NBA players. I swear, if he brings up Muggsy again, I'll go bananas."

Jonesy's life has become a series of tournaments and traveling for games and talk about being ranked nationally as one of the best seventh graders, etc. etc. etc.—which is great and all, but she insists she just likes playing for fun.

"I don't want to go that way! You know me! I wanna study sharks and swim with sea turtles and save the planet!"

This isn't the first time I've heard this rant, but she needs to get it out. I've told her she should have a talk with her dad. She's just . . . working up to it, she says. I actually have another theory.

"Jonesy, you know you can't actually become a mermaid, right?"

I swear that's her final goal. To grow a fish tail and go live under the sea. She's told me she practices holding her breath in the bathtub all the time and she can actually hold it an alarmingly long time.

"Okay." She stops, so I stop. "I know you're joking, but I've been thinking about this. What if I become the world's first 'man-made mermaid'? Somebody has to be the first!"

She's obsessed with some Instagrammers who swim

with sea-life all the time, but this is a new wrinkle. "Explain, please."

"I get a renewable air supply, somehow. And a mechanical mermaid tail. I have a home pod underwater, so I never have to surface? Boom! I'm a mermaid."

I stare at her for a bit before I start walking again. I'm already drawing up the schematics in my head.

Then I shake my head back to reality. "You've been watching too much sci-fi. You'd get eaten by a shark. Day one."

She scoffs. "Whatever. I know how to defend myself. Did you know that if you're getting attacked, you can just punch a shark on the nose? I mean, ideally, you're careful and you never have to—but if one comes at you, just bop him one in the nose. They hate it."

"You're going to boop a shark's nose."

She shakes her head. "Bop, not boop. And it doesn't take

a lot. But you can use an elbow or your foot if you have to. I've seen videos—one pop to the nose and they decide it isn't worth it. All the aggression just goes out of 'em."

I smile. "Okay, Jonesy. Man-made mermaid it is. I hope it happens for you, but it seems even less likely than going pro."

Jonesy actually hops a couple of times, excited. "Can I help it that I'm God's gift to basketball AND the fishes?"

This gets the laugh she was looking for.

Just before our lockers, our path is blocked by a group of football guys doing some sort of elaborate handshake/chant thing. Once they finish—it involved a lot of flailing arms and jumping around—we slide past. And right into a couple of Jonesy's teammates.

"Jonesy Girl!" One of the girls—Kylee (super popular, fun, outgoing, blah blah blah)—makes a happy squeal sound and gives Jonesy a hug. They all three hug, in fact, while I stand there feeling awkward.

Kylee hits Jonesy on the shoulder. "Thanks for talking me down last night, J. I was spinning out. And no, I did NOT call Braden back." They start laughing like she said the funniest thing ever.

Okay. So, they have a little phone-chat club thing going now? Obviously, good for Jonesy, right?—but it makes my nose itch. I should be a better friend than to be jealous like this, but it annoys me. Eventually, the teammates move on. I give them a smile and a wave, so I don't look like a complete jerk.

After they walk away, I can't help myself. I fall on Jonesy's shoulder, fake-laughing like an idiot. "Like, oh my god, J. They are, like, SO funny!"

I see a flash of irritation on Jonesy's face. "Andrew, they're nice. They're cool! They'd like you, but you need to actually hang out sometime—or *say* something—for them to figure it out."

"Okay, okay. Whatever. Duly noted."

Jonesy rolls her eyes while I shake my arms and roll my head around on my shoulders. "Shaking it off. I'll be Mr. Super Social next time."

Our lockers are only two away from each other, which works out great because Jonesy's door sticks. She spins her combo a few times and then steps back for me to do my thing: I bang my fist just below the top corner and yank the handle really hard like I'm starting a mower. It rattles open. She's tried to get the trick down, but it only works for her about a fourth of the time.

"Voila." I spread my arms wide like a magician, and accidentally hit someone's backpack.

She rolls her eyes. "I'm filing another complaint about this thing today. Lockers should open. It shouldn't be rocket science."

When I turn to my locker I notice Danny—the red-headed kid from the bus—standing right there staring at me with a weird look on his face. Like, his eyes look unfocused and his mouth is hanging open a bit and his beloved juice box seems forgotten. I wonder for a split second if he's been zombified.

"Danny? You okay?"

That's when Danny lets out what might be the biggest, most violent, out-of-nowhere sneeze I've ever witnessed. It's like a nuclear explosion.

I feel wind and droplets, and—as a kid who lived through a pandemic—I recoil in horror, jumping backward into Jonesy.

"DANNY!" I'm wiping at my face. "What the heck, man! Cover your mouth! Into your elbow!"

Danny is all apologies. "OMG! I'm so sorry! That came out so fast I . . . I didn't have a chance! Did I spray you?"

I can't help it. This kind of thing—germs, etc.—freaks me out. I think Covid-times made it worse, but it's part of me now.

"Yeah, you sprayed me! You JUICE-SNEEZED me! GROSS!" I don't actually know if this is true, but the thought makes my stomach clench and I look down at my hoodie.

There's no snot, but in some ways it's worse. There

are tiny purple drops of what looks like grape juice all over the sweatshirt. Maybe eight or ten of them. I'm polka-dotted.

"Sorry! I'd just had a big sip!" Danny looks embarrassed. "Grapetastic Geyser. I think some of it geyser'd up my nose."

I'm not *really* mad at him. I mean, I'm mad, but I know he didn't do it on purpose. "So, you're not sick or anything, right?"

"Nope. Just full of juice." He laughs nervously and I see that his tongue is dark purple too.

I turn and give Jonesy a disgusted look. She laughs and I start digging around in my backpack. "Well, this is just great." Then I see the silver lining and give Jonesy a smile with my eyelids at half-mast. "Hey! See that? That's exactly why I put this on!" I tap the side of my head. "Brains, Jonesy. Smarts. The new shirt's all good."

"Actually, there's a spot on the collar."

"Seriously?!?" I grab my collar and try to contort my neck to see it. "Aw, man . . ."

I storm off with my Tide wipe in hand as Jonesy calls after me with a cheery singsong: "Good luck on the math test!"

I grunt.

Seconds later, I'm leaning in, dabbing at my collar in the mirror in the boy's room. It's just a speck, so I still consider it a win. Then Kendrick Stevens walks in. "Anfrew!"

He's called me Anfrew since second grade when Mrs. Long misspelled it on my name tag for field day. It's a weak joke that's overstayed its welcome, but it's fine. And Kendrick is sort of our wild-man/class-clown, so it's just nice that he even knows my name. I always figure he thinks of me as a stick in fussy, anxious mud compared to him.

"What do you have going on here?" He's looking at the spots on the hoodie draped over the sink.

I wipe and check. Wipe and check. "Danny Juicebox juice-sneezed me."

This gets a loud blurt laugh. It's a catchy laugh—the kind that makes you start to laugh as well—and I think it's one of his class-clown powers. At least it seems like a superpower to me. Talking to pretty much anybody other than Jonesy makes me want to crawl out of my skin or hide in a locker. But Kendrick does it as easy as fish swim. He's a natural, and it doesn't seem to make him want to run away screaming at all.

"Yeah, Danny. That kid never met a juice box he didn't like." He watches the door for a second, then takes out a Sharpie and draws a handlebar mustache on his reflection in the mirror. Just because that's what he does. He smiles at his work and then starts washing his hands. "You ready for science today? It's gonna be epic!"

Kendrick is also my lab partner—we were assigned—but I can't think for the life of me how or why class today is going to be "epic." So I just smile and nod. "Yeah, it is. Ha."

"Okay. See ya later, 'Frew!" He spins on his heel, grabs and wads a paper towel in one smooth move, shoots it into the trash can, and is gone. A minute later, I think I have the Grapetastic Geyser spots on my collar and hoodie under control and head to math.

THE JOYS OF SOCIAL ANXIETY
HEART PALPITATIONS!
HELLO?
WHAT??
FORGETTING HOW TO FORM WORDS!
HOBBIN! FLOG MARMIN SHOOP!
SWEATING!
ARE YOU OKAY?
ALL GOOD. I DEHYDRATE FOR FUN.
HIDING OUT IN BATHROOMS!
THEM THINKING I'M POOPING IS SOOOO MUCH LESS STRESSFUL.

4

THE TEST

Mr. Harris - Math

I get to my desk for math with about .0000001 seconds to spare. It literally rings just as my butt hits the seat. Good thing, too, 'cause Mr. Harris is one of those "earn their respect before you earn their friendship" kind of teachers. He's sitting behind his desk with his arms crossed and it looks like he's doing scowling exercises. His comically bushy eyebrows are furrowed.

After the bell there's total silence—one of Mr. Harris's rules. The only sound is a few sniffles and the rustling of people getting No. 2 pencils out of their bags—because it's test time! Yay!

I pull out an antibacterial wipe and clean my desk. I once found a booger on there at the beginning of this class, so someone else who sits here before me is known to wipe boogers. I haven't gone so far as finding out who it is, but I'm not taking any chances. So gross.

You might think my wipe and I would get looks, but people are pretty used to me and my weird routines. For the most part.

Finally, Harris grunts himself up from behind his desk and grumbles something about hoping we all used our study time wisely.

"Before we begin, it says here they're going to be calling students for photos." He looks at a sheet of paper. "Mr. Courtney's and Ms. Jacobs's homerooms are going to be called first, but those are sixth grade, right?"

Elizabeth Brunch, the biggest teacher's pet in our school, pipes up from the front row. "That's correct, Mr. Harris."

Harris nods at the paper for a few seconds before setting it on his desk. "Very good." Then, he walks the room handing out the test to each student. Once we all have it, he tells us to flip it over and begin.

The only reason I'm not a complete stress case about this is that the test is math. Numbers—for whatever reason—kind of calm me down. Jonesy is the exact opposite and thinks my love for math is further proof that there's something very, very wrong with me.

But math makes sense. At least in my brain it does. There's a logic to it. Writing, English class, and art all seem kind of slippery. Like, there's a million rules and yet no rules. Like you're supposed to learn them just to throw them out and be "creative."

But not math. In math those rules are as good as written in stone. I like rules. And if you know them, it's just a matter of focusing and following the steps.

Sorry.

MATH NERD ALERT

I take a deep breath and dig in. The first question is almost exactly like one that was in our homework, so I get that little buzz that says this test may be okay. Question two is easy enough that I wonder if Mr. Harris is turning over a new "nice" leaf.

Everyone jumps a bit as the intercom box on the wall squawks to life and we hear the high-pitched voice of Mrs. Dithers, the administrative assistant. "Hello students: Could students in Mr. Courtney's homeroom class please head to the Annex Room for photos? Thank you!"

I'm just starting to read question three when I feel a gentle tug at my sleeve. Like someone tried to swat my arm and just got cloth. I make sure Harris is deep into his newspaper and turn around—to see Gene the Mean glaring at me. He sits one seat over and one seat back. His big blank shark eyes are right on mine as he mouths at me "Lean back, idiot."

He wants to cheat off my paper and I'M the idiot?

I turn back and try to ignore him. Instantly, I have a

pit forming in my stomach and I keep rereading the first few words of the next question until I feel the point of his pencil jab me. Not hard enough to break the skin, but I jump. I hazard a glance back, and now Gene looks angry.

"Sit. Back." He mouths it as he scrunches his face up and makes pointing jabs with his tiny finger. "Do it."

Now some real anxiety has joined the party. I know the feeling of anxiety like I know the taste of Nacho Cheese Doritos. But unlike Doritos, anxiety is no fun.

It feels like dread. Like something horrible is going to happen. Like my favorite pet just died or an asteroid is slowly coming to destroy Earth—even though none of that is happening. And then the pressure in my chest starts. And my head. And the stomachache. The urge to tap things gets stronger too.

I adjust my glasses and turn my body so it's blocking my paper even more. I'm not letting Gene cheat. No way. I know this is a move that will probably come back to haunt me, but somewhere inside my dumb brain I have strong feelings about fairness. Lucky me.

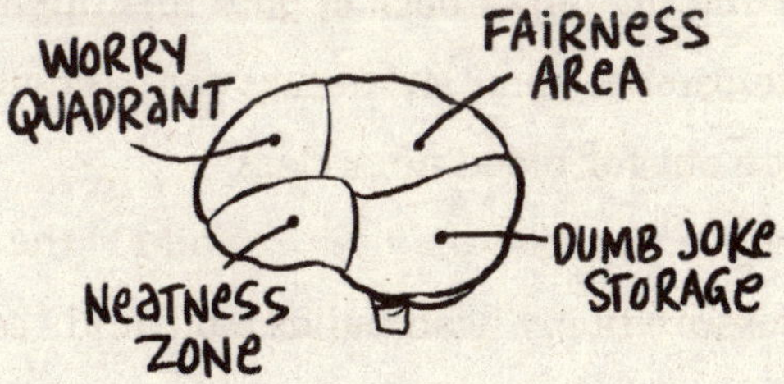

I tap my desk five times, but lightly and under my other arm so no one will notice. I know it looks weird when I do it too much, and the last thing I want to do is look weird. But that voice is in there telling me I need to. Or else. That vague, scary "or else."

I hear Gene clear his throat loudly. Then again. I'm trying to ignore him and get back to my test, but it feels impossible. Like trying to watch videos on your phone with a hungry lion drooling down your back.

The third time Gene clears his throat it's louder and it sounds extra mean—like he wants to murder me. It also finally catches Harris's attention. The newspaper goes down and the big caterpillar eyebrows scrunch even tighter.

"Mr. Phillips. Is there a problem?"

"No, sir. Just a little congested." Gene puts on his sweetest 'Who Me?' voice. "Seasonal allergies, you know. Hay fever." He coughs into his fist.

"Mmm." Mr. Harris is no dummy. He knows who Gene the Mean is. He stares for a few seconds before slowwwwly putting the paper back up and turning back to it.

My attention is shot. My nerves too. I know Gene is going to be out for blood after class.

Ugh.

The pressure in my head builds a bit, and I can't seem

to get the questions in front of me to stick to my brain. It's like my eyes keep sliding over the paper without picking anything up.

Come on. Focus. Focus, focus, focus.

I swear I can hear Gene breathing, not to mention the sound of everyone else's pencils productively scratching all around me. I *know* this stuff. Math is my *jam*. I'm usually one of the first ones to hand my test in.

Come on, A. Stop being a reject and just get on with it.

Not happening. Finally, I set my pencil down and close my eyes. I take some deep breaths—Dr. Cain would be so proud I remember her coping tricks—to try to get the static-y white noise in my brain to shut up. To get that feeling of impending doom in my stomach to loosen up.

When I open my eyes, I adjust my paper so it's perfectly straight on the desk. I line the pencil up next to it exactly. This is another thing that little voice nags me about. Straightening stuff. I put both hands out beside them and take one last breath—then I'm back.

Well. A little bit back. I'm still struggling, but I'm better.

The rest of the test goes like this. I have to keep stopping and closing my eyes to reset. This is taking forever, and I can't stop looking at the clock to see how much time is left.

First, I see Jennifer Mitchell take up her finished test. Then Sawyer Berryman. Then a whole group of kids. And another group.

Then even Gene the Mean! He's ALWAYS last!

Now I can tell I'm the last one working, and I feel like the class is all staring. I have sweat on my lip and my stomach is up in my chest doing some kind of hula dance.

I race through the last couple of questions so fast I have no idea if I'm on the right track.

And then . . . I'm done. I feel kind of barfy and I think I blew it, but I'm done. I walk the paper up to the front, and even gruff Mr. Harris gives me a look of concern.

"You okay, Andrew?"

I fake-smile as I shakily set the test down. "I have no idea."

FUN NICKNAMES FOR PANIC ATTACKS!
FOOMP
BRAIN 'SPLOSION!
FLIPPIN' YER LID
TRAIN CRASH BETWIXT YOUR EARS
FREAK-OUT-A-GEDDON

5

AFTER MATH

Phillips, Gene

When the bell rings to end first period, I throw my backpack over my shoulder and make a beeline for the door. I don't think I actually push anyone out of the way, but I knock into Ashley Swindle pretty hard on the way through the door. I'll apologize later.

I feel a surge of hope as I pass into the cool air of the hallway. Kids are flowing out of other rooms, and I may have a chance at getting lost in the shuffle—but then I feel a sharp yank at my backpack.

Gene.

I have a vision of just slipping out of the strap, leaving the backpack, and running for my life. I could go be one of those mountaintop wise old guys you see in cartoons.

But it's too late. I get spun around and slammed against the wall hard enough that a noise comes out of me that sounds like *gumff*. And then there's Gene's bright red face fuming up at me.

"Are you stupid, Yaeger?"

It's weird having a bully who's a number of inches shorter than you. It doesn't seem right. He literally has to look up at me. But what he's missing in size he more than makes up for in strength, intensity, and untamed anger. I swear he's made of nothing but wire and steel. He also has these cold gray eyes that somehow make him more intimidating. More . . . homicidal.

Like a shark in a Vineyard Vines sweatshirt and sweatbands.

All of Jonesy's shark talk may be warping my brain.

He has the front of my shirt wadded up in his hand and he's pinning me there with a hard fist. My chest was already tight, and this isn't helping.

"No! Sorry! I just . . . You know how I am!" My eyes are darting around the hallway looking for anyone to help, but they're all averting their eyes. "Big rule follower, ha ha. I love me some fairness! Mr. Fair Play!""

He leans in close enough that I can smell his—not great!—breath. "All you had to do was sit back, brainiac. That's all. But you didn't. You wouldn't."

"I'm sorry, Gene. I'm really sorry."

He does this thing where he lets me off the wall a

little and then slams me back with both fists. Does it twice. Then we hear his name.

"Gene Phillips!"

It's loud and coming from down the hall a bit.

I see a teacher's head over the passing students and it's Ms. Wilson. Normally I'm not a huge fan, but right now I could kiss her.

AUTHOR'S NOTE:
NOT REALLY

Gene looks her way and the pressure on my chest lets off just enough for me to scramble away to the side.

Gene feels me sliding away and—risking worse trouble with Ms. Wilson—lunges out at me. He comes in low, maybe hoping Ms. Wilson won't see this part through the crowd. He grabs the first thing his hand hits—the collar of my shirt. He clamps down.

I dart one way and he pulls the other and I hear a ripping sound. I feel it, too, as the collar rug-burns my neck. Chokes me. But I keep pulling. Then Gene lets go and my sudden freedom causes me to stumble down the hall. The only thing that prevents me from going all the way down is the side of the mathlete trophy case hanging on the wall. The top of my head connects hard with the solid piece of wood, making a big hollow *THONK!*

I grab my head, wincing—that *really* hurt—and turn to see Ms. Wilson grabbing Gene by the arm. He's staring back at me with the creepiest grin ever on his face.

"You're dead."

He only mouths it, but I get the message loud and clear. Then he's pulled off into the thinning hallway crowd. Kids are staring, both at me and at Gene as he's pulled away.

My heart is pounding so hard, I can feel my body shaking. I'm mad and upset and embarrassed all at once. I want to scream, but I don't. I guess I'm more of a shove-it-down-deep-inside kid.

I turn around to look at my reflection in the trophy case glass. It's hard to see much, but it looks like the collar of my (brand-new) shirt is all kinds of messed up. I'm furious at Gene, and I reeeeeally wish everyone and their brother hadn't seen that happen—but then I feel a twinge in my stomach thinking of my mom. She'll be so upset. Or disappointed, or whatever.

And none of those kids in G's pile of photos had ripped clothes.

I turn away, gently feeling the top of my head to see if there's a lump, thinking this day is off to a miserable start.

6

GYM CLASS HERO

Coach Shephard - Gym

Looking in the filthy locker room mirror, I see that my shirt is toast. Or at least the collar is. It's all stretched out and torn away from the body part. I close my eyes and let out a long "give me strength" sigh and silently thank my mom for having me bring a spare. (Even if it threw off my entire backpack ecosystem.)

Otherwise I'd be stuck with my faded old too-tight *Gravity Falls* gym T-shirt.

I'm rattled as I change into my gym clothes. It may seem like I'm being a weenie about a dumb shirt, but it's more than that. Things have been *really* tight, money-wise. I know I keep saying that, but you should have seen how excited my mom was when she pulled it out of the bag. It was from Banana Republic! (I gathered from her going on that that means it wasn't cheap and it's super nice.) She'd splurged and felt really good about it.

I think I finally locked in on how much we were struggling financially a while back when she started buying cereal in bags. Like, the ones from the bottom shelf at the grocery store.

That may seem like a small thing, but suddenly we didn't have brand names like Fruit Loops and Cinnamon Toast Crunch. We had generic-looking bags with names like Fruity Yummies! And Cinnamon Squaries! Plus, you can see all the cereal dust in the bottom, which makes any cereal 50 percent less appetizing.

AUTHOR'S NOTE I WILL BEGRUDGINGLY ADMIT THAT DUST AT THE END OF THE FRUIT YUMMIES IS DELICIOUS IN MILK. (IT'S LIKE A CLOWN SMOOTHIE.)

As I walk into the gym adjusting the waistband of my shorts, my thoughts are spinning. I keep trying to think if there was something I could have done to keep Gene calm. Like throwing him a big chunk of raw steak or something.

I mean, I could have just let him cheat. In the grand scheme of things, would that have been so terrible?

Really? All I had to do was sit back. Maybe fake a long yawn/stretch so he could take a look. Why do I always have to be the Fairness Police?

We're playing basketball today, so the gym is super loud and echoey. It's chaos, with a battalion of balls bouncing and flying around as people warm up and Coach Shephard stands under the basket rebounding and blowing his whistle. Over and over. For no reason that I can figure out other than to make the gym even more stressful.

There's another thing: Coach Shephard will not let up on me about basketball. He tells me daily that if I applied myself, I could be "one heck of an asset to the team." It's 100 percent because of my height. Like, that is the only reason. Period. I look like I was born for basketball. Unfortunately, I was born with two left feet. And two left hands. And maybe two left eyes as well. In other words, not in this lifetime. Basketball is Jonesy's jam, not mine.

I walk up beside Tyler Harris. He's a good guy but shy and a little awkward—which has caused him some grief over the years. (From people like Gene.) But, y'know, I'm awkward too, so he's pretty easy to talk to.

He looks over. "Hey, Andrew. Sorry about that."

I think he's talking about the scuffle with Gene—he must have seen it go down. But then it hits me. A horrible smell like bad meat and garbage.

I recoil. "Oh, what the . . . ?" I pull my shirt up over my nose.

"Yeah, sorry." Tyler grimaces. "I burped right as you walked up. You walked right into my Burp Cloud."

"WOW! That is awful—what did you eat?"

"Leftover stew." Tyler shrugs.

"For breakfast?!" I'm moving my head around, trying to find burpless air.

"Yeah. And dinner last night. My mom's taking some kind of online stew class. My house is awash in stew. Chicken stew, beef stew, veggie stew, seafood . . ." I see more than hear him burp again and I've had enough. I turn to scramble away, and that's how I don't see the incoming basketball.

I turn right into its path. I have about a millionth of a second where I see it coming before it slams into my glasses and face and the side of my nose like an orange wrecking ball.

I'm stunned more than anything at first—it takes a few seconds for the pain to register. But I hear a loud *crack* and sense my glasses falling away as I stagger backward. Then another of the eight million basketballs free-ranging around the gym gets in between my feet and I realize I'm going to fall. I go down on my back and elbows. Hard.

I'm still processing it all when Tyler steps in front of me. "Oh, dude!" To me, he's all wavy looking because my eyes have instantly filled with water from the direct hit.

Carter Grier comes running up. "Are you okay?? I really whipped that thing and you walked right—Oh, crap. You're bleeding."

That's when I feel warmth on my lips. I put my hand to my face and realize my nose is gushing blood. Like someone turned a faucet on. I pinch it closed and feel around for my glasses. Tyler hands them to me as Coach Shephard walks up. "Took a pretty good hit, huh?"

No kidding, Sherlock is what I think, but I don't say it. I put my glasses on with one hand, but not before noticing the big Y-shaped crack across the right lens. My stomach drops again. If it keeps dropping like this, it's gonna be in my toes.

The pain is starting to set in. My face is throbbing and there's a sharp sting on the side of my nose.

Coach Shephard does that move where he hikes the legs of his stretchy gym teacher shorts and squats down. He touches my chin in a spot where it isn't covered in blood while taking a look. "Tip your head forward. That'll help with the bleeding." I do, but another gusher of blood shoots out. He looks up at Carter. "Maybe don't stand there like a dope and go get him a towel, Grier."

Through my watery eyes I see Coach lean in close and take a better look. He moves his face around for a while, inches from mine. I try not to breathe 'cause I'm pretty sure his breath would smell like Power Bars and Gatorade. Then I realize I couldn't smell right now if I had to, but whatever.

"Yep. Boy. Noses gush, don't they? Looks like your glasses didn't do you any favors, either. You have a cut there from that nose pad thing. May get a decent shiner out of it too."

Carter runs up with a small white towel. Coach folds it up and puts it gently under my nose. "Hold that there. I think you'll live, but you need to go down and see the nurse. She'll have an ice pack." He gives my arm two hard gym teacher pats and helps me to my feet.

My heart's pounding for a whole bunch of reasons. My glasses. All the blood. A black eye? But mainly it's from embarrassment.

The whole class is standing around me now and all the dribbling noises have stopped. All eyes are on me. I feel my face flushing. Behind me, I hear someone whisper to someone else, "I'd have just *caught* the ball."

It got me good. A perfect shot. I've started wandering slowly toward the door with my head back when I hear the coach.

"Harris, walk him down there so he doesn't run into a wall. And hustle back."

Tyler catches up with me at the door and opens it. As we walk through, he asks how I'm doing.

"I'm fine." Then I roll my eyes over and look at him. "Just please don't burp on me again."

I hear Tyler chuckle as he puts a hand on my back to guide me.

STAGES OF MY ANXIETY
JUST FINE
WHAT NOW?
UH OH. NO.
I DON'T LIKE THIS!
CAN'T BREATHE! GAHHH!
RUN. BACK FAR AWAY.

7

FIRST AID

Nurse Finnegan

As we make our way down the hall, Tyler starts whistling, quietly. He's a big whistler—and actually pretty good at it as far as whistling goes. I think he's just doing it to fill the silence, but I'm actually glad to not need to make small talk.

The pressure is building in my chest and shoulders.

Maybe I'm filling up with blood and I'm going to burst like a tick. (That thought doesn't help.)

Unfortunately, this is a familiar feeling. I've had it in varying degrees for years, and a global pandemic didn't help matters. It's anxiety. I've even had two panic attacks, but those are . . . awful. I don't want to talk about those.

Anyway, here's how anxiety feels. For me, at least:

Imagine you're a kernel of popcorn.

You're just chilling out in the bag, hanging with your buddies, and then you get dumped into a pan full of slippery oil. No biggie, right? It might even feel good at first. But then . . . the heat starts to rise.

It rises slowly, so at first you don't notice it. You're just toasty and warm and hanging out being a kernel.

Then you start to feel a little uncomfortable. Like when you wear a sweater that's too heavy and you can't decide if you should take it off or not.

But then . . . you're more than warm.

Then you're downright hot.

And with that heat, this weird pressure starts to build

deep inside you. And it keeps building up. You start looking around for a way out but, y'know, you're a kernel. You can't move.

Now you're really starting to sweat, and there's this PRESSURE. An internal pressure. It feels like someone is trying to inflate you, but there's nowhere for the air or pressure or whatever it is to go.

You (the kernel) twitch a few times. Maybe it starts to feel a little like panic.

This pressure has to go SOMEWHERE. Are you going to explode?? Is that a thing?? Can you just . . . POP?

It just keeps building and building and you twitch some more and you're freaking out and you can't breathe and there's nowhere to go 'cause it's all inside you and you can't take it anymore and . . .

Okay. It's like that, kind of. Anxiety, that is.

(I don't even want to talk about the panic attacks yet. When I had my past ones, I . . . I kind of freaked out. At least they didn't happen at school. That would be . . .

Nope. Can't happen. Can't even imagine. Honestly, the panic attacks I had were horrible and scary and messy and teary and devastating, and . . . No thank you. Having one of those at school would be a Very Worst Nightmare Scenario. Worse than the one where I realize I'm naked in class times ten million.)

So, the kernel thing—that's what it feels like now. Like I'm in hot oil and I might pop and the feeling is building inside me and I can't get away from it.

I even came up with a little sliding "Kernel Scale." That's how I think of it in my head. Here's where I am as I head to the nurse's office.

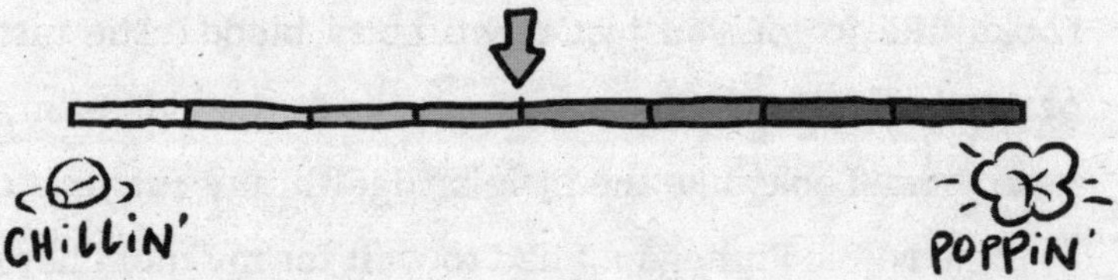

I know, I talk about anxiety a lot. Sorry. But I also know "There's more to me than just the anxiety." My therapist, Dr. Cain, says that a ton. It's just . . . something that comes up a lot.

So, I'm thinking about stages and kernels and hot oil and exploding all over the walls when we get to the nurse's office. Tyler knocks and we hear the school nurse call out for us to come in.

Nurse Finnegan is typing on her laptop when we walk in. She glances up and sees Tyler at first. "Back for more antacids? Maybe your mom's stew class should—"

That's when she spots me, behind him, with the bloody towel and shirt. She gets up quickly, sending her stool rolling away.

"Uh-oh. What do we have here?" Tyler steps aside as she comes over and takes the towel from my nose.

"Basketball vs. Face," Tyler says, and I'd give him a dirty look if I didn't think it'd restart the nose-gushing.

Nurse Finnegan gently takes my glasses off. "Wow. Looks like it got you just right. Lotta blood." She just barely touches my cheek as she looks at the side of my nose. "Mm. Looks like the little bridge-thingy cut you."

I like Nurse Finnegan. I had to wait for my mom here once when I came down with a stomach bug, and even feeling barfy with a bucket in my lap, waiting with her was kind of fun. She seems like there's a cool big sister hidden just under her nurse persona. And, just like today, she was wearing bright red Converse low-tops with her scrubs, which seemed kind of cool.

(Do all school nurses wear scrubs? Or is that a Nurse Finnegan thing? I wonder.)

A few minutes later, I'm lying on the office couch and Tyler's been sent back to class.

Nurse Finnegan tries calling my mom but gets her voicemail, as I told her she probably would because she's hyper-focused on her new job and probably has her phone on silent and tucked way away.

I have cotton balls in my nostrils, an ice pack on my eye, and Neosporin on the cut on my nose. She helps me sit up enough to take a sip of water with a couple of Tylenol. The cold water feels and tastes good.

When I lean back, I close my eyes and let out a long sigh that kind of turns into a frustrated growl.

Nurse Finnegan sits down on her rolling stool. "You okay?"

My head is pounding and the tension in me is threatening to spill out. I say what I'm feeling. "No."

"Yeah. You've looked better." She rolls over and wets a few paper towels in her sink. "I hope that isn't your only shirt. It looks like a Jackson Pollock painting."

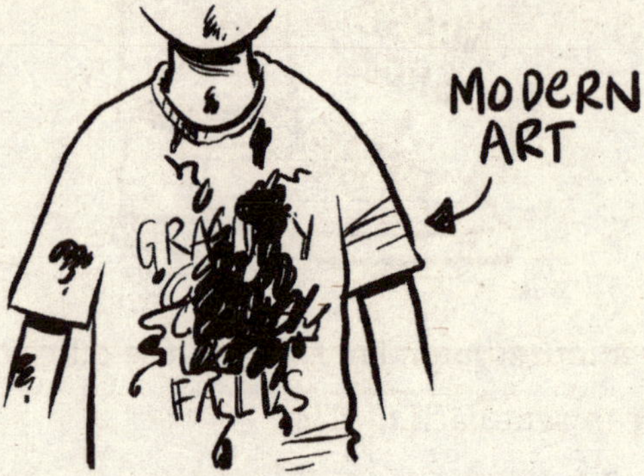

I don't know who Jackson Pollock is, but I open my left eye enough to look over at her. "That's two shirts ruined today. Not that I'm counting."

She asks, so I tell her what happened to the other one, and about how my mom had just bought it for my pictures.

She lets out a one-puff laugh, but it's like a laughing-with-me-not-at-me laugh. "Well, when we're done, bring it by here. I can't promise anything, but I was in charge of sewing and fixing all my brother's clothes growing up." She rolls her eyes.

"Okay. Thank you. That'd be awesome." I lie there with my eyes closed for a minute while she carefully wipes some blood off my chin and neck. "Am I going to have a black eye?"

"Hard to say, but it's kind of looking that way." She's

lifting the ice pack for a look when the door starts to open. A booming, singsongy voice calls out "Hellll-looooo? Miss Nurse Lady?"

I look up as Mr. Kellerman—the art teacher—comes to a quick halt when he sees me on the couch. His eyes dart to Nurse Finnegan and I swear he blushes.

"Whoops. Sorry." He laughs a little, awkwardly. "The door was ajar, so I didn't think you had anyone—" He looks back at me, and I see him take in the bloody clothes, the icepack—all of it.

"Wow. Andrew? You okay?" He sounds genuinely concerned. Mr. Kellerman is hands down the coolest, funniest teacher in the school.

"I've been better."

Nurse Finnegan drops some bloody paper towels in the giant trash can in the corner. "Basketball injury. We may have to amputate the head."

Mr. Kellerman chuckles and twirls the end of his mustache. This is such a Kellerman move—chuckling and twisting his 'stache—that it's how I'd imitate him. He's a big guy with a big beard. He's kind of a brown-haired younger Santa type—if Santa wore overalls and flannel shirts and socks under his sandals. I've heard my mom call him "quite the character."

"I'm sorry to hear that. It's a pretty decent head, as heads go."

I close my eyes, trying to get my nerves under control.

"Well . . . hey. I have to run some errands. Want me to pick you up something for lunch?"

At first, I think he's talking to me, so I open my eye again. He's looking at Nurse Finnegan and she has her mouth twisted up, thinking.

"Will you be near the deli? I'd love that smoked turkey thing I had last week."

Now, THIS is interesting. Are these two . . . dating or something? Do teachers date? Is that allowed?

"Yep. Going right by there. Jalapeño chips? Diet Coke, light on the ice?"

She points at him. "You know it."

"Okay." Mr. Kellerman looks over at me and there's an awkward pause. "I'll see you in art class, Andrew. Don't die."

I nod. "I'll try."

Then he backs out of the room and it's just the two of us again. I look over at Nurse Finnegan. "What was *that*?"

A weird grin slides over her face. She rolls over to her laptop and punches a few keys. "You just close your eyes and heal, Mr. Yaeger."

But she's still smiling when I put my head back. And for a few brief seconds I haven't thought about being a kernel in hot oil.

Fifteen minutes later, I'm walking back to the gym—and not looking forward to the attention. I just need to duck into the locker room, change, and then run my new shirt back down to the nurse's office.

Of course, when I open the gym door, everyone stops and turns. Coach Shephard has a basketball under his arm as he yells out, "Hey hey!! Yaeger lives! What's the prognosis?"

I yell back, just loud enough to be heard, "Just . . . she said to change clothes and . . . head back down there. More ice."

Coach nods his head a few times. "A'ight. That's fine. But we're working on free throws tomorrow. You can't get away from me that easy!" He laughs, turns, and blows his whistle again for who knows what reason. I'm relieved when everyone turns back to what they were doing.

On my way to my locker, I stop at the mirror. Leaning in, I see that I'm already starting to bruise around the cut where my glasses got me, but there's a faint purpleness starting to spread as well. I lean on the sink for a few seconds, wondering how hard it is to Photoshop out a black eye.

Why couldn't I have been in that first group to get their photos taken?

I let out a five-second sigh.

Six minutes later, I'm back at the nurse's office—in my extra shirt and with a fresh ice pack on my face—while Nurse Finnegan inspects my collar.

"Boy. It's almost all the way off." She's trying to line up the collar with where it's supposed to be. "Absolutely no promises, but I'll see what I can do." There's a little sewing kit and some scissors on the couch beside me.

"Thanks."

She stares at me for a few seconds. "You all right?"

"I'm fine."

She's still looking at me. "You keep tapping your finger. You've done it a bunch of times."

My heart lurches in my chest. I'm usually pretty good about hiding that. I hadn't even realized I was doing it. "It's just a thing. A thing I do." I don't go on about the anxiety and the two panic attacks or my mom taking me to Dr. Cain and the sketchbook and all, hoping the subject will go away.

"Mm." She's nodding. Little nods that barely move her head, like she's thinking. "Well. I'm always here if you want to talk."

Thankfully, the bell rings and I'm free. I thank her and she sends me off with the ice pack wrapped in some paper towels.

Time for Social Studies. I sit by Jonesy, so maybe she can help me turn this day around.

COOL SIDE EFFECTS OF ANXIETY!
MAKES INTERACTIONS EXCITING!
TICKETS
ONE TICKET, PLEASE?
YOU'RE GONNA HAVE TO SPEAK UP, CHILD!!
GETS YOU NOTICED!
THAT KID'S A MOVER AND A SHAKER.
WELL, HE'S SHAKING, AT LEAST.
QUIVER
WORRY
FRET
MAKES YOU EAGER TO TRY NEW THINGS!
CAMP?
NO.
SPORTS?
PASS.
BAND?
NOT MY JAM.
CLUBS?
HARD PASS.

7.5

DAWN OF THE SKETCHBOOK

Dr. Cain (I Google'd her photo)

The first look I got at Dr. Cain was when she poked her head into her waiting room. She was a lot shorter than I'd expected a therapist to be—shorter than Jonesy, even—and had a head full of gray-blonde curls so tight, they looked like they hurt. If I'm honest, she reminded me of a hobbit, from Lord of the Rings. (My mom and Mika love those movies, so Jonesy and I kind of do too, I guess.)

I don't mean that hobbit comment in a mean way—it's just what jumped into my head. I mean, she didn't actually have furry feet or anything. At least not that I could tell. But instead of shoes, she was wearing these big puffy socks that my mom always gets for G in her stocking at Christmas. I think they're called cabin socks.

That struck me as weird right off the bat.

"Hi. Are you Andrew?"

I closed the travel magazine in my lap. I'd been staring blankly at an article on the Ten Most Breathtaking Pools in Guam. "Yeah."

She smiled, and it was a calming one, which was good. I was pretty nervous.

"Hi Andrew. I'm Dr. Cain. Why don't you come on in."

My mom stood up with me. "Do, um . . . Do you want me to come in with him, or . . ." She made a face and a funny little dance with her hands.

Dr. Cain looked at me. "That's up to you. At some point I want to talk to you alone, but we can start with your mom or call her in after a bit?"

I had no idea. I didn't really want to be there anyway. I shrugged, rolled the magazine into a tight tube, and made a choice. I felt like this doctor's job was to examine my every move and judge it, so I didn't really want to look like a wimpy little kid who needs his mommy with him.

I looked up. "Maybe we call you when we need you?"

My mom nodded and smiled, gave me a quick hug, and held her hand out for the magazine.

In the office, Dr. Cain shook my hand and told me to take a seat. There was a couch and a couple of big chairs.

Was this a test? Had the analyzing started already? Like, do only messed-up people take the chair on the right? If I chose the left one, am I a bed wetter or a future serial killer or something?

I cleared my throat and sat in the chair on the right—just because it had padded arms.

Dr. Cain went over and moved a few things on her desk until she found her pen, grabbed a small legal pad and settled into the big chair across from me. She crossed a leg, clicked her pen open, and gave me a warm smile. I had to break my eyes away from her fuzzy red-and-white-striped socks. I did notice a pair of brown shoes over by her desk. I guess there's nothing wrong with a cozy therapist.

"Hi."

"Hello."

"How are you doing, Andrew?"

This was weird. I felt the pressure in my chest and shoulders tick up a notch and fought the urge to tap the arm of the chair. Or to hose it down with an antibacterial spray. (I didn't know who'd sat here.)

I knew she was watching me closely—like a brain

detective. I looked around the room as I thought of how best to answer that. It was decorated tastefully, as my mom would say. Big leafy plant. Abstract print over the couch. Box of Kleenex at arm's reach in case I started bawling. Photo of Dr. Cain and her husband and two daughters by the printer.

Then I noticed something I wished I hadn't. Under one end of the frame, there was something—I couldn't tell what it was—just a little crumb or a tiny dead fly or something. It was small enough that a "normal person" would never notice it. But boy, I sure did. It had that end of the frame up just high enough that a thin sliver of light was coming through under the frame, and it just . . . wasn't right. Suddenly it was all I could see in the room and all I could think about.

I remembered she had asked me a question, so I pulled my eyes from the crumb/bug thing. "You mean, how am I doing in general? Today? I'm . . . nervous, I guess? Tense? I've never done this."

She nodded and smiled again. "Well, I figured you hadn't."

My eyes shot back to the frame. It being crooked was kind of making me itch. All over. I wanted to go fix it so bad, I felt like my brain was twitching.

WHAT LOOKING AT THAT CROOKED FRAME FELT LIKE TO ME
ANTS CRAWLING ALL OVER ME
TWITCH
UHHH
SWEAT
LIKE THE ENTIRE WORLD IS CROOKED
IS THAT NOT BOTHERING YOU?
WHAT?
LIKE THE FRAME IS MESSING WITH ME
LOOK AT ME, KID!
LOOK AT ME!!!
C CRUMB
A CRUMB-TASTROPHE!
RUMBLE RU
AAA!

Finally, she noticed my eyes darting back and forth to the frame.

"Is . . . is there something about that picture that has your attention?"

Busted. Ugh.

Now I felt exposed. I hung my head and waved a hand at the frame. "There's a crumb or something. Under the edge. I know it's stupid and weird, but . . . can I go fix it? It's gonna bother me until . . ."

It flashed through my head that maybe this was a trap. Maybe she puts this crumb under there before every new patient to sort out the true wackos. But she just got a surprised look on her face.

"Oh, I hadn't noticed!" She hopped up and grabbed a tissue and took care of it. Her eyebrows went up when she looked at me. "Better?" And mercifully, it was. The frame was straight. She looked down into the tissue and laughed. "Ah. Part of an Oreo. A client yesterday had her toddler with her. She was eating cookies and moving my stuff all around. Thanks for catching that."

She tossed it in the trash and my body relaxed to pre-crumb levels.

She sat back down and waved the toe of her big sock around a few times.

"Please don't be nervous. We're just going to talk for a bit. You can't do anything 'wrong.' There are no bad answers. I'm not testing you or anything."

My eyes must have reacted, because she let out a silent laugh. "Everybody thinks I'm testing them. I hear it from all my new patients. How they feel like they're a bug being studied. Analyzed. *Dissected*. But it's really not like that."

I nodded and shifted around to get more comfortable. She pointed at my chest. "What's that shirt?"

I looked down. I was wearing my Cowboy Ross and the Loading Dock Misfits T-shirt.

"It's a band. Some kids a couple years ahead of me. They're in high school now." I didn't tell her I'd found the shirt in the bottom of my sixth-grade locker.

She smiled. "Very cool." Then she clicked her pen in and out once. Like a restart. "Your mom says you're dealing with some anxiety. And maybe that's coming out—showing itself—in some different ways?"

I nodded again, looking at the colorful art print. The three blobs looked somewhere between frogs and ghosts and big boogers.

"Yeah. I feel, like . . . pressure."

She waited. "What kind of pressure?"

I sniffed and looked at the ceiling. I wasn't trying to

be weird, but it's hard to talk about it. It's personal. It's *embarrassing.*

"Sometimes it feels like . . . I don't know. Like pressure in my shoulders. Or . . . like there's electricity in them. Or sometimes it's in my head or my chest. Or sometimes my stomach freaks out from it."

She was writing and not staring at me, so I figured I must be doing okay.

"It's . . ." This is a thought I'd had before but never shared. "I think . . . it's like that feeling you get when you're excited for something—like Christmas morning, but you have to wait. Like that buzz you have in you when something's coming that you can barely stand. But instead of it being a *good* buzz, it's a *bad* buzz. Or like . . . tension. And sometimes there *isn't* anything coming. I just feel . . . that way. Does that even make sense? I know that's . . . whatever."

She looked up at me. "Actually, that's a really interesting description. And it sounds . . . hard to bear."

I kicked my feet around for a bit.

"So, then I . . . I freaked out a couple of times. And sometimes I tap things. Flip the light switch. Check the door a bunch. Stuff like that. And germs. They kind of make me . . ." I waggled my fingers to end the thought. "That's why I'm here, basically."

"Okay." She took a few seconds to write something down on her pad.

"Can you tell me more about the freak-outs?"

Oh boy. Straight for the big stuff. I took a deep breath and spoke quickly as I let it out.

"It was . . . like all that pressure, but then it . . . it got way worse and worse and then . . ." Sorry for all the dots, but it was hard to figure out how to say it. "Then it was more than a buzz. It was a *BUZZZ* and a roar and all the electricity and pressure and I . . . felt like I was about to die." I was looking around like I was gonna find the right words on her carpet. "I couldn't breathe . . . and my chest was crazy heavy and everything *looked* weird and I felt, like . . . like a wild animal . . . and my chest hurt and then I kind of crashed and I cried a bunch."

She nodded for longer than you'd think, looking at me kindly? *Nicely?* "That must have been terrifying."

"It was." I let my breath out and relaxed my shoulders and looked back out the window. "And now I'm . . . always worried that it might happen again. Like, now that I know how horrible it is, I worry that it might get that horrible again. And that makes me worry and worrying makes me worry more, and . . . on and on." I looked down and I was rubbing my arm without realizing it, like I was cold. "So . . . you know . . . it stinks. I worry all the time that I'm gonna freak out again, especially while I'm at . . ."

I tapered off and tapped my finger five times on the armrest.

I didn't care if she saw—I'd already told her I do it. In a way, it was nice not to have to hide it.

Dr. Cain looked up. Watched the taps. "You're worried you'll have another panic attack while you're what?"

I blinked. That was the first time I'd heard anyone call what I had a "panic attack." I mean, I figured—I know how to google symptoms online—but to hear a professional say it was weird. Maybe a good weird? Like, it was a real thing and I wasn't just being ridiculous? My mom had always tried to play it down and called it an "episode"—for my sake—but now I knew.

"While I'm at *school*. I can't . . . I can't even imagine that. Don't want to." A Panic Attack at School was now my Number One Biggest Fear in the Universe. Still is. In my mind it looks like me sprawled on the floor crying and squirming around and who knows—maybe I pee myself—and the entire school laughing and pointing at me. I know that's a bit far-fetched, but my innermost brain doesn't seem to think so—it keeps serving that vision up to me.

"Yeah, I can understand that." She raised her eyebrows and jotted a couple of things down. "Can I ask what brought these episodes on?"

"Um . . . different things."

She smiled. "Okay. Like what? What made these things different?"

I hadn't really thought back on those times. On purpose. They weren't fun to think about, so best not to, right?

"One was because of my grandma, G. She was . . . I mean . . . she was acting weird. Alzheimer-y weird. Not like herself. It's so dumb and not important what actually happened, but she was making me late, and making things difficult. She locked my bedroom door—I mean, it's her bedroom now, but I have stuff in there that I need. And she was scared 'cause she didn't . . ." My eyes were filling with water at the memory. "She didn't know who I was. She was yelling. My mom wasn't home. And it just went on and on and got worse and worse and it just . . . There was nothing I could do and I couldn't calm her down and . . ."

If you could pump pure kindness out of your eyes, that's the way Dr. Cain was looking at me.

"It felt like a nightmare. Like I was trapped in a nightmare and I couldn't . . . I couldn't wake up. *Life* was the nightmare."

Dr. Cain waited a second while I took a few deep breaths. "Wow."

I laughed a not-funny laugh. "Yeah. Wow."

I sat back, so she asked, "What about the other time?"

"The other one was dumb. I don't even want to . . ." I didn't want to go into that one. "It was nothing that should have . . . panic-attacked me. It was just . . . a super long dinner with people I didn't really . . . It was stupid. But it *felt* the same. That nightmare feeling, and that pressure and that buzz and then I lost my . . . lost my handle on it, or something. It just took off like an airplane. I couldn't help it. It was . . . really, really awful. It makes me feel sick to think about it."

Dr. Cain had a bunch more questions for me, but she took her time. She assured me she could help prevent these things from happening and give me some things to do if they were to happen.

She asked if I thought those were two situations where I felt like I didn't have control. I nodded, sure. Then she wrote a bit more on her pad while I stared out the window.

"Okay. And the tapping? Does it make you feel better? Does it make you feel more in control?"

I shrugged. I knew it wasn't a great response, but I'm really not sure if it does.

"Or do you just . . . feel like you have to, or something bad will happen if you don't?"

My eyes shot back to her. I'd never told anyone that. I always feel like something terrible—some awful unknown thing—will happen to my mom or G if I skip these little tasks. Check and recheck that the apartment door is closed and locked. Flip the switch three times. Tap five. Count my steps. Straighten stuff on the counter. Fix the corner of my sheets. It gets exhausting. It's like an all-day version of that game Step on a Crack, Break Your Mother's Back has taken over my brain. (And if I'm honest, I always make sure to never step on cracks. Ever. And if I accidentally do, I worry that I'm going to get home to find my mom crumpled on the kitchen floor.)

How could she know that? About the "Something Bad" thoughts? About the little voice.

"It's actually not that uncommon, Andrew. Lots of people have things they do like this. I see it all the time. And I've helped lots of people." She's holding eye contact like she wants this to sink in. "I hope just knowing this will make you feel better."

I found myself nodding. "Okay."

"You're going to be fine, Andrew. We can work on this. The tapping. The anxiety. The attacks. All of it."

I nodded some more and for some reason felt tears filling my eyes. I blinked a few times and looked away to clear them out.

"How about you tell me a bit more about you? Can you tell me about your life?"

"Okay. Like . . . what?"

"Whatever you think. Just tell me a bit about Andrew Yaeger." She leaned back and folded her hands like I was going to read her a good story.

I wasn't sure where to start. I cleared my throat and shifted around again.

"I'm . . . twelve."

Dr. Cain started writing on her pad.

I was trying to think of what was important. "I'm going to be starting seventh grade after the summer. I live with my mom and my grandma, G."

Slowly, I started telling her about stuff.

Sometimes, she'd stop me and ask questions back, like when I told her my parents got divorced five years ago and my dad lives on the West Coast and we pretty much never hear from him.

"Oh. I'm sorry to hear that. That must be hard. How do you feel about it?"

I thought about it for a second. "Lousy? I guess? Angry? I mean, I remember him, obviously. I remember him being mad a lot. Really mad." My nose itched and I rubbed it with the back of my hand. "He was a jerk to my mom. And me. I try not to think about it 'cause it gets me angry and upset and then I feel like . . . him." I felt that twitch of anger and aggressively wiped at my nose. "I think it's better that he isn't around."

She'd stopped writing and was looking right at me. Completely still, like she was thinking.

"Does that make me weird?"

She shook her head. "Nope. Not at all. I'd say you

have a pretty sophisticated take on the whole thing."

I wasn't sure if that was a compliment, or if I should thank her, so I just looked back at the frog-booger art.

Dr. Cain got super interested in my grandmother's Alzheimer's and her moving in, as well as when I talked about Jonesy's new basketball buddies and school and all that stuff, and when I talked about how I mow a bunch of lawns around town to make money after school, and then I just kind of . . . ran out of things to say. But she said I'd done great. It was a great start.

That's when we called my mom in.

For a while, it was just them talking about how therapy works. Dr. Cain said there might be times when my mom would join us, and times by myself. She wanted to set up a schedule, which they did, but I'd heard my mom telling Mika on the phone that morning that she could probably only afford a few visits. Something about terrible insurance. But there in the room she acted like that wasn't an issue.

AUTHOR'S NOTE:

I WENT THREE TIMES,
BEFORE MY MOM- ALMOST
IN TEARS- TOLD DR. CAIN
THAT IT WAS ALL WE
COULD MANAGE RIGHT THEN.

After all that, Dr. Cain went over to her desk and came back with a black notebook about the size of a Captain Underpants paperback. She handed it to me.

"Okay, Andrew. This is for you. It's a sketchbook . . . notebook . . . whatever you want it to be."

I flipped it open. It had blank, unlined pages. There was an elastic strap to hold it closed that looked kind of cool. The cover had one word pressed into it. *Moleskine*.

I looked up at her, grossed out. "Is this made of moles?"

She laughed. "That's just the brand name. I'm really not sure why. I think it's French or something."

She sat back in her chair. "Here's what I want you to do, Andrew. I want you to write and draw in this book. About your anxiety, about how it feels. About anything. Every day, okay? Can you do that?"

"I can't draw."

She shook her head. "Doesn't matter. Draw stick figures. Or scribble. Or just write, but I think both writing and drawing what you're feeling can be really helpful.

Try it. I won't be judging on talent. I won't be judging at all. In fact, you don't have to show it to me if you really don't want to. But I think you might surprise yourself."

I looked at the book in my hands for a minute. "What if the idea of writing or drawing about my anxiety gives me anxiety?"

My mom and the doctor looked at each other. "Try not to overthink it. This is for your eyes only. Just promise me you'll try it."

I nodded a few times. "'K."

"'K." She tapped her knee with her pad like she was wrapping up. "Find a good pen too. Something that feels 'different.' That can help. Maybe your mom can run you by Michael's on the way home."

My mom rubbed my arm. "Absolutely." Then she grabbed her purse, stood up, and that was it. That's how the session ended.

As we walked to the car, I actually did feel a tiny bit better. It felt like something had begun. It must be how people feel in a crisis when they know the paramedics are on their way.

At the car, my mom stopped before unlocking it and looked over the roof at me. "What'd you think?"

I looked around the square, then back at her. "It was okay, I think. Her socks were kind of . . ."

She smiled and hit the fob. "Well, they looked comfy to me. Let's get outta here."

We did stop by Michael's on the way home and I got something called a Micron pen—a couple of them, in different line weights actually. The scruffy-looking guy working there recommended them. Then my mom and me and my sketchbook and my Microns headed home.

Here's the first thing I drew.

Not really a drawing, I guess. And "Not Great, Bob" was from some meme I'd seen online a bunch, but it seemed like an okay start.

I started doing The Anxiety Files a few days later. I tried making them like some of the Instagram comics I follow, though mine aren't always funny. I'll settle for funny-*ish*. Or at the very least, honest.

WHY DO I TAP STUFF??
BECAUSE I HAVE TO.
TAP TAP TAP
IF I DON'T, SOMETHING AWFUL WILL HAPPEN.
TAP TAP TAP
THE WORLD WILL BLOW UP, OR...
TAP TAP
OR THERE'LL BE AN ACCIDENT OR SOMETHING.
TAP TAP
AND THEY HAVE TO BE GOOD TAPS. ALL FINGER, NO FINGERNAIL.
TAP
IT'S A LOT OF RESPONSIBILITY.
DID YOU DO YOUR HOMEWORK?
CAN'T. SAVING US ALL.
TAP TAP

8

NOTES AND SUCH

Ms. Bayer - Social Studies

I slide into my desk next to Jonesy. She looks up from doodling a sea turtle on her folder and her smile freezes. If my eye weren't throbbing and puffing up and I weren't so full of dread, the moment would be kind of funny.

She takes it all in, her eyes getting bigger. The ice

pack, the darkening eye, the broken lens of my glasses, the different shirt.

"Did you fall off the roof?" She looks genuinely concerned.

"I wish." Other kids in the class turn around to look at me.

"Seriously, what happened?" She leans in to get a better look at my eye.

I sigh. "A rogue basketball happened."

"Wait." She sits back again. "That was YOU?? I heard some kid got nailed in the face in gym and had to . . . How? A *basketball*?? They're full of air!"

This isn't improving my mood. "Yeah. I'm aware. It was a one in a million shot. Lucky me." I give an exaggerated smile, but it makes my eye hurt.

Jonesy keeps staring with her mouth open, and finally a laugh comes out in spite of herself. She puts a hand over her mouth. "I'm sorry. It's not funny. But, wow! Where's your shirt? And is that *blood* on your arm?"

I turn my hand over and see a spot Nurse Finnegan missed on the outside of my wrist.

"Yeah. My nose gushed blood like a fountain." I say it quick and low. I can tell the kids around us are listening as hard as they can.

"WHY WERE YOU WEARING YOUR NEW SHIRT IN GYM?"

The bell rings as I start shaking my head. "No. Unrelated. I bled on my *gym* shirt. Gene ruined the new shirt."

"Gene?? What??" Jonesy's mouth falls open again as Mike Winslow turns all the way around in his seat, fully engaged now. But Ms. Bayer is clapping her hands to start class.

I gesture at Jonesy to calm down, but she's still gawping at me, confused. She waves her hands around in the international symbol for "What the heck?" She mouths it too.

I scribble my hand in the air and go for a piece of paper out of my folder. As more homerooms (that still aren't mine!) are called to the annex for photos, I find half of the last English quiz in there. I'd used the other half to wrap up a huge wad of Hubba Bubba last week. I flip it over and write in the corner.

GENE TRIED TO
CHEAT OFF ME. I
DIDN'T LET HIM. HE
DIDN'T LIKE THAT.

I fold the paper and slip it to her when Ms. Bayer has her back turned. Jonesy reads it and rolls her eyes practically to the back of her head. She starts writing and hands it back a couple minutes later.

So, he what? Ate your Shirt? Also, how do You get a 78 on this quiz?? It was So easy!

Dang. I forgot my score was written on the bottom of the sheet. And for the record, that quiz was NOT easy. I write back and even add a little drawing:

PINNED ME IN THE HALL. TORE THE COLLAR OFF. NURSE F TRYING TO FIX.

Jonesy reads the note. First, she shakes her head, then smiles when she sees the Gene drawing. She's writing something back when the classroom door opens. Ms. Bayer stops her lecture—about political parties or something—and turns. We all turn, and in step Principal Espinosa and Gene.

Gene immediately spots me and starts glaring with the watchful eyes of a murderous velociraptor. He's messing with his wristband, like he really wants to do some punching.

"Hello, Ms. Bayer," Mr. Espinosa says in a bright, cheerful voice. He's our slightly round, friendly, overly polite principal. He's just this year bumped up to principal from assistant principal and he's very enthusiastic about the new gig. "I was wondering if I might have a word with Andrew Yaeger in the hall. You have *my* word I'll have him back in a jiff."

"Oh, of course!" Ms. Bayer gestures with both hands at me like Vanna White. (The letter-flipping lady on *Wheel of Fortune*. G likes it.) Everyone is watching me as I stand up. My legs feel like they're made of Silly Putty. I see some mouths open in O shapes and someone makes the dreaded *Ooooooh* sound. Jonesy just looks surprised.

At the door, Mr. Espinosa and Gene lead the way. Mr. Espinosa closes the door and it's just the three of us in the hall. Next to a locker, across which someone has scribbled:

TONY DON'T EVEN KNOW

No, he don't, I think—as my anxiety kernel starts to heat up. We've gone up a notch, for sure.

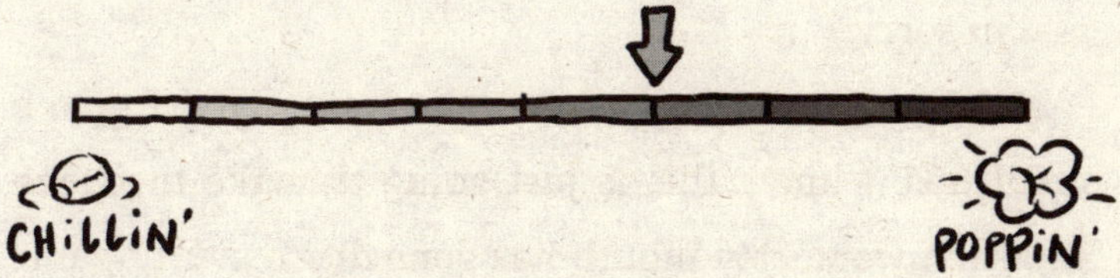

Gene has his arms crossed as he leans against the locker. Now he's looking anywhere but at me.

I like Mr. Espinosa, but . . . am I in trouble? He's always been really nice to me. He actually had my grandma for social studies back when he was a student, and he's told me he liked her a lot. He always asks how she's doing.

"Hello, Andrew. I'm genuinely sorry to bother you in class, but the events of earlier today were brought to my attention, and I felt the situation required an immediate intervention." This is how he talks, I swear. "I heard about your unfortunately damaged shirt from Ms. Wilson. Gene, do you have anything you'd perhaps like to say to Andrew here?"

Gene looks at me and then Mr. Espinosa. "That I'd *like* to say?"

Mr. Espinosa has his hands on his hips. "Gene."

"Fine. I'm sorry. Whatever." He tips his head back like he's asking the ceiling for strength.

Espinosa isn't satisfied. "Now might we try it without the attitude?"

"I'm sorry."

Mr. Espinosa looks at me, eyebrows up, and I give a small nod. I know this is just going to make the Gene Situation worse. My mouth has gone dry.

He has us shake hands. I have the urge to dunk my hand in Purell. Maybe my whole arm. I don't like any germs, but these are Jerk Germs. Extra nasty.

"Okay. So . . ." The principal puts his warm, damp hand on my shoulder. "We've discussed this, Andrew, and we've left messages with both your and Gene's parents, as neither answered. We've explained that Gene here will be purchasing a new shirt for you. A replacement. The *same* shirt, Gene. Are we clear?"

Gene stares off down the hall and gives an almost nonexistent nod.

Mr. Espinosa seems pleased. "There will also be a

commensurate punishment—although I haven't yet decided quite what that will be. I'll inform you by the end of the day, Gene." Then he shakes his head—at the whole situation, I guess. Or maybe he's wondering why he became a middle school principal in the first place.

"Thank you, Andrew. I'm so terribly sorry this all transpired." Seriously, he said "transpired." "Gene, I'll be escorting you back to your class now. And then I'm trying your dad again."

I could swear I see Gene wince at that.

Five seconds later, I'm back in my seat and I can feel the eyes of the class on me.

My eyes would be on me too. I sit back, cross my arms, and stare straight forward—intent on looking at nothing and no one. My basketball-smashed eye really hurts and it's getting puffier, and my cracked glasses lens is annoying and my heart's racing and I have that creeping worry that this could spin out into a full-blown Panic Attack and no, no, no, no. That can't happen here. I mean, I've never even told Jonesy about the two full-blown freak-outs.

I'd really love to just crawl under ten or twelve heavy blankets and go to sleep.

Finally, after ten minutes of riveting political talk, I chance a glance over at Jonesy. She's looking right at me and has the paper from a straw crumpled up and hanging from one nostril. And she's making this face she makes where she lets one eye go partly cross-eyed.

I can't help it—it gets a laugh out of me. Then she scrunches her nose up really hard and it gets another laugh.

My kernel in oil breathes just a tiny bit easier for a few seconds.

9

LUNCHABLES PT. 1

Another delicious well-balanced cafeteria meal

As soon as the bell rings, Jonesy is all over me for details.

"What happened? Tell me everything. What did Gene say? Is he getting detention? Is he going to murder you?" She has a basketball under her arm, which is weird for the middle of the day. But it comes in handy as a prop. She holds it up. "And how did . . . ?" In slow motion, she brings it toward my face as she makes a whistling noise like an incoming missile.

I fill her in on everything as we head to the cafeteria. Fortunately, we have the same lunch period. I'm not usually hungry this early in the day, but whatever. Jonesy's always hungry.

When I get on the other side of Jonesy, I see she's had someone draw another mermaid tattoo on her right shoulder. This is a thing she does. She'll let anybody Sharpie a mermaid on her. This one is one of the worst.

"You do remember it's picture day, right?" I tap the horrible artwork. "Who did this one?"

She laughs. "Reagan. That girl can't draw to save her life, but I still kind of like it."

We turn the corner and we're hit by the smell of School Food. Ugh. It always smells the same. Like a combo of tater tots, bad pizza, Salisbury steak, waxy red apples, and spoiled milk. And it's strong enough that I can smell it through my blood-crusted nose.

I bring my own food, thank you. So does Jonesy.

We sit at the round table by the vending machines. They used to have good stuff in there—like cinnamon rolls and Doritos—but recently the school board people seem to be on a health kick. They're full of high-protein snacks and fruit and stuff now and nobody goes near them.

We sit down and—after I thoroughly clean the table with a wipe, of course—start pulling out our lunches. Mine from a crumpled paper bag and Jonesy's from a fancy little Thermos brand box with a whale embroidered patch on the front. Sure enough, my PB&J comes out of the bag looking like a sumo wrestler used it as a sparring partner.

Disgusted, I'm peeling it carefully out of its smeared plastic bag, while Jonesy is telling me about all the tournaments and games her dad has scheduled for her this weekend and how excited he was to meet some guy from the Michigan women's basketball program and wondering if she should have the "I just like to play 'cause it's fun" talk with him.

"I . . . I just don't know if I can do it. He thinks I can get ranked nationally. He spends all of his free time thinking about it and talking about it. It makes me sick to tell him that I really just want to play for fun. I feel like he'll get upset or mad or—ugh—heartbroken. I don't think I can stand to see the disappointment in his face. It might break *my* heart."

I take a tentative bite of my mushy sandwich and talk through the mouthful. "Do you want me to talk to him about it?"

Jonesy freezes, looking at me. "Seriously? You'd do that?"

I nod and take another bite. "Sure. Your dad loves me. We get each other. I think I could tell him in a way he'd understand."

She looks genuinely shocked. "That never even crossed my mind. That wouldn't make you nervous? It makes me wanna barf, just thinking about it."

I nod. "Sure, it makes me nervous. But your dad and I are buddies. We've had some pretty good 'man to man' talks. I know how to get him laughing."

Jonesy's mouth is literally hanging open. "Andrew, I will owe you forever if you do this for me."

"Pssssh." I make a face at her. "Jonesy, do you know how much I owe you? Heck, you taught me how to ride a bike! And pretty much how to swim. Or at least swim better."

She smiles. "Yeah, but you did teach me to do an underwater flip. I wouldn't be much of a mermaid without that."

"Jonesy, you're also just my best friend in the world. Of course I'll talk to him. I think we're coming to your house Friday for dinner. I can do it then."

Jonesy puts her hands together. "Oh. My. God. Thank you so much, Andrew."

That's when Kylee and another teammate of Jonesy's walk up, smiling.

"Hey, Jonesy. Andrew." Kylee sees my face and pauses like she lost her train of thought. "Are you okay, Andrew? I actually saw that whole thing with Gene. He is truly the worst."

I feel my cheeks start to turn red. "I'm okay."

Jonesy talks through a smiling mouth full of sandwich. "Oh, Andrew here is having quite the day. Got into it with Gene and then with a speeding basketball as well!"

Kylee makes a face. "Ouch. Well . . ." She shrugs. "Basketballs can be hard."

I'm not sure if she's being sarcastic, so I just cram more PB&J in my face.

"We just wanted to see if you want to come sit with the team, Jonesy?" She gestures with a long thumb to the other side of the cafeteria. "You too, Andrew. There's a couple of seats open."

I look over at Jonesy. When she pauses, I jump in. "Oh, we're . . . I have a couple of things I need to talk with Jonesy about. Got a whole agenda, ha ha." I pat my folder like there's an actual printed agenda in there. Why am I being such a brat about this? Kylee is being nothing but friendly.

Kylee smiles. "No, that's cool! Totally get it. We just wanted to offer. You're welcome anytime."

Jonesy gives a big smile. "Thanks so much! Maybe tomorrow!"

Then Kylee and the other girl—Melissa—are gone, and Jonesy punches me in the arm. Hard.

"Ow! Maybe you *could* punch a shark!"

"What is your problem? They're super nice—and they're always nice to you as well. Why do you have to be like that?"

I shrug. "Sorry. I just thought we were . . ." That's all I say. Weak, I know. I don't want to tell her that the idea of going over there and talking with the team tenses my entire body up. Just the two of us is so easy.

"I'm sorry, but all that talk about hair products and hot dudes would really put me off my sandwich."

She stares back for a minute. She looks kind of irritated and I feel that in my stomach. "You can be snotty sometimes. You need to work on that."

I shrug and say I'm sorry again, but we've had plenty of conversations. She knows I'm not a snob—just uncomfortable around new people sometimes. We eat in silence for a minute. Finally, I change the subject.

"Why is anyone that uber-rich such a jerk?"

Jonesy knows I'm talking about Gene and shakes her head. "I have no idea."

"If I was loaded like him, I'd be the happiest guy in the school, y'know? I'd walk around giving high fives and handing out twenties. Or fifties!"

Jonesy nods. She seems to have let the Kylee thing go. For now. "Between us, my dad has done some business with Gene's dad and thinks he's a horrible human being. So . . . maybe it's hereditary. In his DNA, or something."

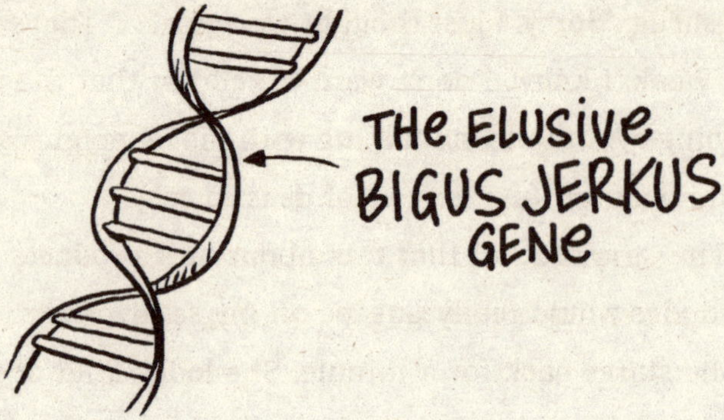

She continues. "Guh. I heard him going on about how expensive his new shirt was yesterday, by my locker. His new *salmon-colored button-down*. He must have called it his 'salmon-colored button-down' about ten times in a minute. And flipping his hair around. He's a ridiculous combo of fussy and terrifying."

Just then, Kendrick, the class clown/my lab partner, comes up to our table. "Anfrew! Whoa! Check that eye! You're turning all the colors of the rainbow." He leans in for a closer look. "I'd heard about it, but dang. Looks good on you, though."

I give what's probably a weak smile back.

Kendrick bumps my shoulder. "Hey. Listen. Can I borrow your ketchup bottle?"

"Please. Take it away." I find ketchup repulsive. I know I'm in the minority, but I do. The smell, in particular. I push it over to him. He picks it up and seems to weigh it in his hand.

"Perfect! Thanks, man. Bummer about your glasses."

Then he's gone.

We're quiet, mouths full, when Jonesy jumps a bit and looks at her Apple Watch. "My mom's calling. Weird." She starts digging in her pack for her phone. We can have phones in school, but they have to stay in our bags or lockers. (All I have is G's old Jitterbug phone that my mom gave me for emergencies. It's a phone for old people that only has certain stuff on it. Like, you can pretty much only use it as a phone. I'm embarrassed enough by it that I never take it out. It's somewhere—battery long dead—in the bottom of my locker, I think?)

"Mom?" Jonesy wedges the phone between her shoulder and ear. "What's up?"

She nods and looks over at me. "Yeah. Right here. Okay. Hang on." She holds the phone out to me.

I stare at it, confused, so Jonesy shakes it a bit. "She wants to talk to you."

Huh?

I grab the phone. "Hello?"

Immediately, I can tell something isn't right. Mika sounds out of breath. "Hey, honey. How are you doing?"

My inner popcorn kernel's oil temperature bumps up a degree.

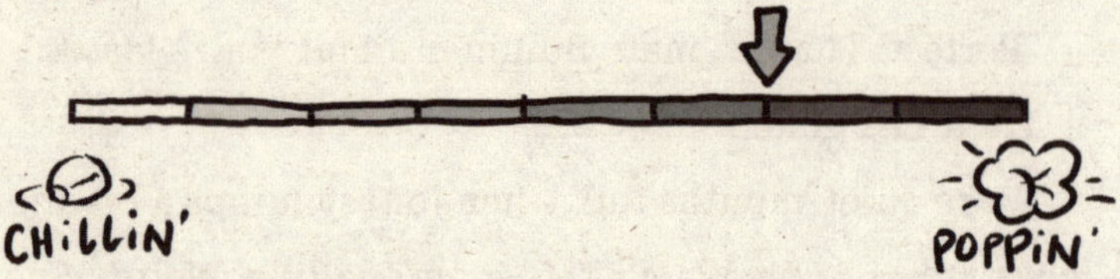

"I'm fine. Is something wrong? Is it G?" Anxiety sinks its long teeth into my shoulders.

She takes a deep breath and lets it out in a *whoosh*. "I'm sorry to bother you, Andrew, but . . . (frantic sigh) . . . I can't find your grandma, honey."

10

WAIT, WHAT NOW?

My stomach drops what feels like ten stories and I sit up straight. "She isn't in her room?" Jonesy's eyes get bigger, alarmed.

"No, honey. She was in there sleeping all morning. And now she just . . . isn't there. I mean, I went to the bathroom, but . . . ? That's the only time I can think of when she could have gotten past me. She's not in the hallway or downstairs. I looked around outside."

"Have you called my mom?" I'm standing up now, and walking toward the windows. Toward outside. Toward cool air. I need air.

"I tried, but she's not answering. She's probably so busy with her new job and her new boss or has the ringer turned off or—"

"Okay." I close my eyes and put a hand on the windowsill, feeling unbalanced. I feel a flash of anger at Jonesy's mom, but I shake it off—and start tapping. Five taps on the sill. Five taps on the window glass. Kendrick has everyone at the table behind me laughing hysterically about something. I try to tune them out. "Should you call the police?"

"I have, Andrew. They're sending someone. That's part of why I'm calling. I know she's wandered off before. Is there somewhere in particular she likes to go? Somewhere we should look first?"

My chest feels so tight, I have to stop and think about breathing for a second.

Another notch. Almost in the red now.

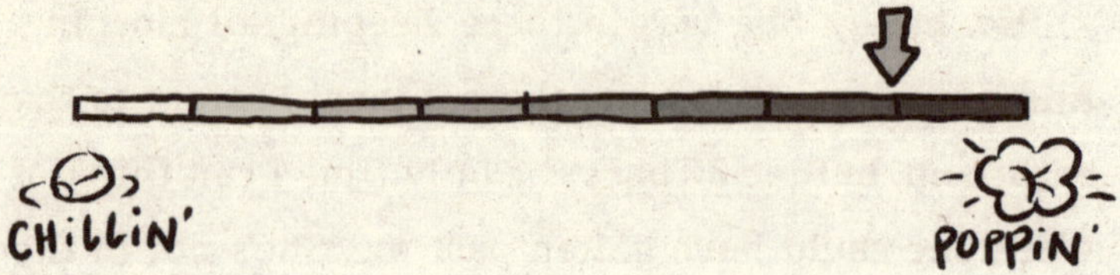

"She likes the pond. The apartment pond. The geese and herons and . . ." I feel Jonesy beside me. "Or check the Donut Den on the corner? She used to . . . I don't . . . Or . . . she loves McDonald's. She talks about Egg McMuffins all the time. Check there?"

I push open the door to the small patio outside. Students are allowed to hang out there during lunch. I pass the DO NOT LEAVE THE CONCRETE AREA! sign in the window. The outdoor furniture is in the process of being replaced, so there's nowhere to sit. With that and the day being kind of drizzly, nobody is out there except two gamer kids sitting on their raincoats stealthily playing Switch with their backs against the wall where teachers can't see them. (No video games in school.)

Jonesy follows me out.

"Okay, Andrew. We'll check those spots first." Mika sounds like she's outside as well. "Now, listen to me. I'm so sorry to upset you with this. Everything is . . . it's going to be fine. The police are coming. I'm here. I'll keep trying your mom. And G can't have gotten far, okay? I wasn't in the bathroom that long." I think I hear a faint siren in the background—would they run the siren for a missing Alzheimer's patient? Maybe the sirens are going off inside my head.

Mika goes on. "So, just . . . hang in there. Let us handle

this. I'll call the front office now, and I'll let Jonesy and the school know the very second we find her. Try to stay calm."

Like staying calm is a choice.

"Okay. Are you sure you shouldn't come get me?"

"No. I don't want to take that time. She has to be around here."

I nod a bunch. "Okay." Somehow, I feel numb and like I'm on fire at the same time. An early drawing I did in the sketchbook comes to mind:

"The police are pulling up, Andrew." There's relief in her voice. "I have to go. Remain calm. Everything is going to be okay and we'll laugh about this later."

She hangs up and I stare at the phone for a few seconds. Jonesy is watching my face. She puts her hand on my arm.

"You okay?"

I feel like there's a blue whale (the largest of all mammals, I think for some reason—probably a Jonesy fact) crushing my chest, and my shoulders have that buzzy, too-much-electricity ache and I'm shaking a little as I look back at her, reaching for the right words.

No. No attack. No panic attack. Not here.

"I . . ." My breath shudders out of me like I'm cold. "No. Not okay. I don't feel okay at all."

10.5

THE WANDERER

This isn't the first time G has wandered off. I mentioned that time she drove off to Indy, but she's done it a few times on foot as well, since she moved in. One time we found her by the apartment dumpsters. One time she was on the swings at the complex two over from us.

My mom calls them Housecoat Escapades when she's talking to G. It sounds funny, and I think she's just trying to keep things light, but there's nothing funny about them. She'll be like "Mom? No Housecoat Escapades today, okay?" Sometimes G'll smile. Sometimes she just keeps staring out the window.

But it's scary.

I talked about G's escapes with Dr. Cain. About how weird it is to have this woman who partly raised me be so not herself that we have to watch her like a toddler. How my mom's been looking at childproof locks for the front door to protect G from herself. (Now I wish we'd already installed them.) I made a joke that we could get one of those dog tethers from her leg to the couch, but my mom didn't find that amusing.

We've had two Late Night Search Parties, in fact. Zero fun. Do not recommend. Unless wandering around in the pitch-dark with flashlights, worried, is your idea of a good time. It's stressful, and exhausting, and then no one can get back to sleep and you're all stressed-out zombies the next day.

I guess the one upside is that G always seems to be in pretty good spirits when we find her. Everyone else is panicked and rattled and near tears, but G always seems like she's just fine. Especially that time we found her on the swings.

Sometimes I wonder what she's seeing in her head when she goes on her adventures.

Finding her all blissed out and unaware can honestly be pretty irritating—although it's better than finding her freaking out or crying or hurt or something. That would be awful. I really hope nothing bad like that ever happens. I mean, obviously.

Dr. Cain asked me once what the hardest part of having her live with us was.

I started to slide my fingers under my leg to stifle the

need to tap—but then just let the tapping happen, as Dr. Cain is well aware of it. Hiding it is a habit.

I thought for a second. "The guilt?"

"Guilt about what?"

"About being super hugely crazy annoyed by her?" I did five more quick taps on the chair cushion for that statement. Dr. Cain saw it and gave me a comforting smile.

"I feel bad. I mean, she's G, but she's also so, so not. And it's just . . ." I looked around the room trying to find the right word. "Inconvenient! I feel terrible saying that—I really do—but it is!" There was a whininess in my voice that I hated.

Dr. Cain nodded. "Tell me more about that part. The inconvenience."

I sighed. I felt the anxiety kicking around in my chest, and then I just . . . unloaded.

"Okay. I mean . . . She has *my* room now, right? And . . .

You can't keep the daylight out of the front room where I sleep. It's those thin white plastic blinds and they don't keep the sun out at all and there aren't drapes or anything to close so I wake up with ***blinding light in my eyes every morning*** and I tried hanging a *blanket over the window* but it bent some of the stupid blinds and my mom went on about the damage deposit and ***I just want my room and my bed back***! The pull-out couch has this *bar* in it about halfway down that isn't that bad at first *but by two or three in the morning it starts to really hurt. And then G gets up and wanders around at like, four a.m. and she hums and rubs her dry hands together loudly or she sits down on my feet and sometimes she'll turn on the TV—loud—or sit there on the end of the bed eating her graham crackers dropping crumbs everywhere and I'll try going back to my room but my room smells like* **old person** *now—and pee and farts if I'm being completely honest—and that's just* ***gross****, and it skeeves me out even though it's my grandma who I love and then I just end up awake. And we have to* ***hide things*** *and* ***keep things away from her****—so I feel like we're living in some kind of weird* ***prison*** *and I can't even talk to her like I used to when she was awesome and she's* ***ALWAYS THERE*** *and I have* ***ZERO PRIVACY*** *and* ***sometimes I have to change my clothes in the kitchen if***

she's in the bathroom forever*—and I mean* ***FOREVER****. It's weird.* ***Try changing clothes in your kitchen sometime****— it doesn't feel right.* ***No one should be naked next to their stove. Ever.****"*

I stopped and that last naked stove comment hung weirdly in the air. I realized I was out of breath. Like I'd been holding my breath for a year.

I wasn't done, I guess. "Sorry. It's just . . . ***THREE TIMES*** *she's accused me of stealing her stuff, and she gets*

really, really mean about it and calls me a little jerk and a thief like she doesn't know who I am, and I get it—I know she really doesn't. I mean, I know that isn't her, it's the disease, but *I hate it. She yelled at me for a* ***whole day*** *that I'd stolen her pillows—like I'd want her stupid smelly pillows—and* ***do you know where we found them?*** *Under the sink! With all the cleaning chemicals and sponges and junk! She'd crammed 'em in there!"*

*"And she's not '****there****' enough to admit she was wrong or say she's* ***sorry*** *so she just goes back to stinking up my room and waking me up eating graham crackers and leaving her gross mouthguard thing on my toothbrush and . . . getting in the way. She's just . . .* always in the way."

That last part felt like I went too far, and I kind of wished I hadn't said it. "Does that make me a huge brat?" I ran a shaky hand through my hair.

"Not at all." Dr. Cain smiled, her hands in her lap. "Frankly, it sounds like a real pain in the ass."

I laughed. One quick blurt. I hadn't expected her to say that.

She went on. "Seriously, Andrew. That sounds really, *really* hard. Being out of your room, in particular. Between you and me, crawling into my bed at the end of the day is one of my very favorite things. I look forward to it." She smiled and closed her eyes for a second like she was dreaming of bedtime. They popped back open. "And privacy! Seriously! *Everybody* needs privacy! Especially at your age."

I calmed down a bit. "Right? I mean . . ." I wasn't sure what else to say. I'd been annoyed for so long—and convinced I was being a World Class Horrible Jerk for feeling that way—that this felt weird.

"Andrew, you're describing an *incredibly* difficult situation. Anyone would be put out. And frustrated." She set her pad on the little side table—we were near the end of the session. "Alzheimer's is really, really, really hard. Maybe most of all on the care partners. That's you. And your mom. If you weren't uncomfortable—or annoyed or angry or sad or stressed out—that's when I'd be worried. You're just being human. And sometimes being human can be incredibly hard."

For some reason this made me think of aliens.

"My advice is to go a little easier on yourself. Maybe a *lot* easier. Cut yourself some slack. Let yourself off the hook, all right?" She smiled. Then she checked her wrist-watch and gave me that "I hate it, but we're out of time" look. "And maybe get some air freshener for G's room. Or some incense?"

That got another small laugh from me. "Febreze. Got it."

WISH LIST FOR MY OVERREACTIVE BRAIN
The ability to take it out of my head for a little break.
YOU CHILL HERE FOR A WHILE
Maybe get it a sleepytime tea and a soothing massage.
OH, THAT'S THE STUFF
Take up meditation or something.
Please!
OM.

11

LUNCHABLES PT. 2

The cafeteria's spacious outdoor dining patio

We're still on the concrete lunch patio, just off the phone from getting the news that G is missing, and Jonesy is trying to meet my eyes.

"Andrew? You good, buddy? You in there?"

My cheek twitches as I run a hand through my hair. "Yeah. I'm here. I just . . ." I flutter a hand in front of my chest. “Can’t breathe. Need more air.” I know this feeling. I’m terrified I’m heading into Panic Territory.

Jonesy glances over at the two gamers, who I’m sure are eavesdropping on us by now. “Well, we’re outside, so . . . more air is tough.” She gives me a hug. “This is all gonna be okay. I bet G’s back on the couch watching *The Price Is Right* ten minutes from now. She may be kind of a ninja when it comes to sneaking off, but she’s not great at hiding, you know?”

“Yeah.” I start nodding. “I hope you’re right. I just feel like there’s got to be something else I can do. Somebody else I can call.”

Jonesy holds me out at arm's length. "Andrew, I'm telling you, my mom is good at this stuff. Remember when we went to Kings Island and I wandered off? Remember she somehow got on the *loudspeaker*?"

A tiny smile hits my lips from the memory. "Yeah, she went full Mama Bear. I think she scared some of the staff. Especially the kid dressed as Scooby-Doo."

"Right?" She laughs. "So, let's let Mama Bear Mika do what she does best. She'll tear the town apart."

That image makes me start to smile, but it feels like my cheeks are shaking. Jonesy notices.

"Can you do your breathing thing? To calm down?"

It's one of the things I've shared with her about my meetings with Dr. Cain. She gave me a few breathing exercises, but one worked the best. She called it box breathing. I was skeptical until she told me that Navy

SEALs do it to stay calm. I decided if Navy SEALs do it, I could give it a shot too.

I nod and start up.

First, you breathe in through your mouth for four seconds. I do, and the breath quivers a bit as it goes in.

Then you hold your breath for four seconds. This can be really difficult when you're spinning out. I count it out in my head.

Third, you let your breath out through your nose for four seconds. I turn a little away so I'm not breathing peanut-butter-scented nose air on Jonesy.

Then you wait for four seconds before starting it over. And you repeat it as many times as you need until you feel yourself calming down.

That's all it is. It's pretty easy. It seems stupidly simple, but it really has helped, sometimes. Dr. Cain showed me a little box diagram where the four-second parts are the four sides of the box.

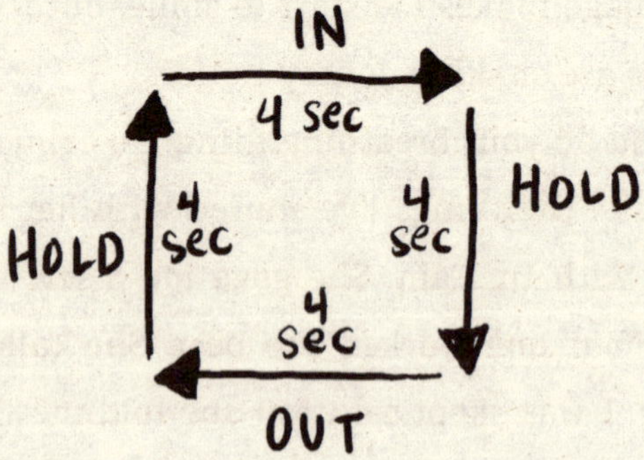

I turn all the way around, facing a big wet shrub of some kind, and do the breathing pattern a few more times.

Four in. Hold four. Out four. Wait four.

Finally, I turn around and Jonesy has her eyebrows up. "Better?"

"Maybe. A little?" I think I went down a notch. Maybe two.

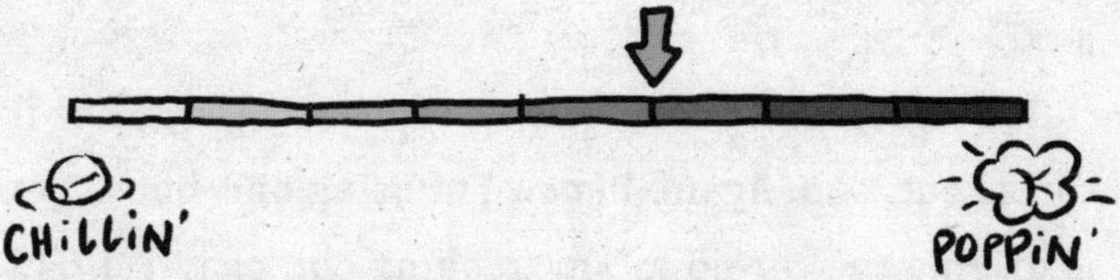

That's when the gamer kid closer to me—I think his name is Jackson?—speaks up. "Yo, are you having, like, a heart attack or something?"

Jonesy turns and shoots him a look. "He's fine."

Jackson shrugs and goes back to his game just as I feel a raindrop land on my arm. And another on my cheek. Then the cafeteria door opens and Kylee sticks her head out the door.

"Hey, is everything okay?"

My mind is almost all on G, but now I'm kind of annoyed too. I'm an irritable live wire right now, and . . . if I'm completely honest, I'm probably just embarrassed to have anyone else see me this way.

"We're fine, Kylee. Thanks so much." The words are nice enough, but they come out sounding rude. Sarcastic.

Kylee makes an "oops" face and puts up a hand. "Yep. Sorry." And she backs inside, closing the door. I feel bad. I really do. I'm being a jerk, and I know it.

Jonesy spins on me. "Why?"

"What?" I play dumb.

"I know you're upset, but why do you have to be a jerk?"

Too many things are on top of me. "I'm a jerk?!" It comes out loud. Again, I *know* I'm being one, but anger is driving the car now. "I'm freaking out, okay?!" I flail my arms out like G and my hands smack into the wet bush. "My grandmother's missing! Did you forget that??"

Jonesy looks wounded. "What? No, of course not, Andrew."

I can't stop. "And what about your mom? What about Mika? Your mom can't keep her eye on one old lady? How hard is that?? She was probably too busy online-shopping, buying fancy throw pillows and Ultra Smoothie machines to watch G!"

This was too far. It didn't even make sense. I mean, her mom loved nice stuff, but that's hardly a crime. Jonesy looks like I punched her in the stomach.

"You're being mean."

I'm not myself. She's right. I'll admit that. I'm half me and half anger.

"Whatever. Go tell Kylee about it. But be sure to tell her how your mom lost G."

Jonesy's eyes are wet as she backs up, turns, and darts through the door. There's a voice in my head screaming at me that I'm being horrible and to take it all back, but it honestly felt kind of good to let some of it out. Angry Andrew feels kind of like he won.

Won what, I have no idea.

I rub at my face and look around. That gamer kid Jackson is watching me.

"That was harsh, man."

I let out a disgusted rush of air in response and go for the door. I step into the cafeteria and immediately know something is up.

People are yelling and laughing and leaning forward—

some are standing on their chairs—looking at a table in the middle of the room.

That's when I see the source. Kendrick jumps back from the table, just as a plastic ketchup squeeze bottle—the one he borrowed from our table—shoots into the air, spraying an aggressive stream of ketchup behind it. Half the cafeteria lets out a loud yell of "KETCHUP ROCKET!" as the bottle goes straight up, hits the edge of a ceiling tile above it, and changes course.

Toward me.

I turn and curl up, covering my face. The bottle shoots over me and hits the door behind me with an echoing *THOCK* sound.

The cafeteria erupts in cheers and applause.

I straighten back up, and for a few seconds, I'm checking myself for ketchup. My shirt: clean (at least the front is). My arms: clean. But I can smell it. So gross. That's when I reach up and feel the stickiness in my hair. Then the smell hits me and I almost gag.

I grab some brown napkins from a table, and I'm dabbing at my hair when Kendrick comes up. He has tears in his eyes from laughing, but also looks concerned.

"Hey, are you okay?? That was friggin' amazing, but I'm sorry it came at you. It got in your hair?"

I'm mad, but I'm mostly grossed out. "What was in there? Is it bad?" All I need is some chemical to burn my hair off.

"It's all household stuff. Baking soda. Stuff like that. My cousin told me how. It's a chemical reaction, but it's harmless stuff." It'd be really nice if Kendrick put this much effort into our graded science experiments.

He grabs a few more napkins and hands them to me. "Sorry." He's smiling, but then it fades for a second as he darts a look over his shoulder, then back to me. "We're good, right? You won't tell anybody it was me? I'm kinda hoping everybody just . . . clams up. Like *'We don't know what happened! The school musta bought faulty ketchup bottles!'*"

I make sure he sees the death glare I give him.

Someone walks by and yells "SO EPIC, Kendrick!!"

Then I hear the boom of Mr. Abrams's voice at the door. "WHAT HAPPENED IN HERE?" He teaches eighth-grade science and is *not* a teacher to mess with.

Kendrick hears this and gets an "uh-oh" look on his

face. He hands me another napkin and pats me on the shoulder. "Gotta run. See you in class." He darts away and expertly blends into the group of students by the door.

I look at Mr. Abrams. He's leaning back—hands on hips—looking disgustedly up at the dripping streak of ketchup across the cafeteria's tiled ceiling.

Then Tyler walks up, chewing, holding a Tupperware full of what I can only assume is his mom's stew.

12

THE MENDED COLLAR

Back to another bathroom mirror, and I don't like what I see. Smelly nasty ketchup, drying in my hair. So gross. And my black eye is pretty much swollen shut at this point. Maybe the cracked lens will distract people's eyes before they get to the shiner. At least there's nothing on my clothes. It's miraculous, really.

I put my head down and lean on the sink, doing my breathing thing for a minute. I can't believe I was a jerk to Jonesy.

It's like my stress over that and the G thing (and my current ketchup-haired state) are teaming up on me. My stomach is killing me. I hope I don't have a blow-out. (It happens. Stress can do that.)

During one of my grandma's first Housecoat Escapades, I heard my mom say she was worried we'd find G "at the bottom of a ditch somewhere." I wish I hadn't heard that, because now that's exactly what I picture every time we don't know where she is. It's what I'm picturing now. It's a vivid image: G lying next to an abandoned tire and some fast-food trash in a flooded roadside ditch. Although given how unconcerned she seemed when we've found her before, she'd probably be happy as a clam down there.

That thought doesn't make me feel any less like barfing.

I'm thinking about this as I start using wet paper towels to clean the thickening ketchup out of my hair. Did I mention I hate ketchup? Pretty sure I did. The smell and the feel of it is making me want to hurl. Quickly, I realize I'm just going to have to go for the full head-under-the-faucet hair-wash situation.

Hoping no one comes in, I take off my busted glasses and then my shirt—suuuuper carefully so it doesn't touch ketchup hair—and fold it neatly, setting it aside. It's a small sink, so there isn't much room, but I get some moderately warm water going and manage to wet all my hair with only a couple of minor head wounds from the metal faucet.

Unfortunately, when I'm done, I realize that wetting it down just intensified the ketchup smell.

I smell like Ronald McDonald's cologne.

I look at my options for "shampoo." There's that awful school pink liquid hand soap in the dispenser—but it smells craaaazy strong and somehow "institutional."

I've always thought it smells like perfumed gasoline. Not an option.

There's also a hand sanitizer dispenser. I know from experience that it smells way better than that nasty institutional soap. It even has a bit of a coconut scent added in.

I grab a couple squirts and rub it into my hair, then rinse it out. I have a passing thought that the alcohol content might make my hair fall out, but then an image of G in that ditch pops into my head and I let it go.

I grab a handful of brown paper towels and do my best to dry my hair a bit. The bathroom feels cold after the shampoo job.

Looking in the mirror at the shaking, black-eyed wet rat I've become, all I can think of is that picture book about that poor kid's terrible, horrible, no good, very bad day.

I feel you, Alexander.

I use my fingers to try and comb my hair, but it isn't behaving. It's sticking out all over. I put my shirt back on and head for the nurse's office. I keep my head down in the halls, hoping I'm invisible.

Nurse Finnegan takes one look at my messed-up, wet-hair-dripped-on shirt and her hand goes to her chest. "What happened now?" She has my shirt in her lap and she's fiddling with the collar.

I look over at the small mirror on the wall. "I got ketchup'd."

"Seriously?" She stares for a second. "You aren't doing this on purpose, right? It isn't some viral online Picture Day Challenge or something?"

I sit down on a chair in the corner. "It is not."

She holds up my new shirt and smiles. "Well . . . your timing is good, at least. I've just about got this thing fixed. I ran out of thread, so I'm just figuring out how to safety pin the . . ." She looks up and her smile fades. She must see something in my eyes. "Hey. Are you okay?"

I sit for a second before I shake my head. Then I shake it again and oh man, here comes that sting in the nose and behind the eyes. Tears are on their way. I look up at the ceiling to stop them. "No." I hear my voice quiver as I say it and I'm embarrassed. I take a couple of deep, slow breaths. "It's a bunch of stuff. All this . . . stuff. Mostly it's my grandma."

She comes over to sit in the chair next to me. She starts rubbing my back as I tell her about the call from Mika. And about the Alzheimer's. I tell her all of this while I stare at a poster on the opposite wall of a cartoon hedgehog washing his hands.

She assures me everything will be fine as I nod and think of course that's what you're supposed to say to a kid in this situation. But nobody really knows, y'know? It's just words.

I feel my shoulders tightening and—I don't really have a choice—I tap the little metal cart next to me five times. I do it quietly and down behind my leg, so she doesn't notice. She's focused on the poster too. We're both staring at the hygienic cowboy hedgehog.

"Andrew." She sighs. "I'm sorry you're having a wreck of a day. I truly am." She's quiet for maybe ten seconds before she speaks again.

"Do you like Flamin' Hot Cheetos?"

This catches me off guard. I sniff and look over at her. "Yeah, why?"

She smiles. "They're kind of my secret vice. I claim to be a healthy eater—I'm a nurse after all—but I can't help it. I love 'em." She sets the shirt aside, stands up, opens a cabinet, and pulls out a basket full of little bags of Flamin' Hot Cheetos.

"Secret stash. Don't tell anyone." She holds the basket out. "Want some? Like, before you put the good shirt back on. No offense, but you and shirts today . . ."

I give a weak smile and grab a bag. I do, in fact, love Flamin' Hot Cheetos, but my mom refuses to buy them.

"You don't think they'll burn my insides out like my mom does?"

Nurse Finnegan shrugs and carefully plucks a Cheeto out of my bag and pops it in her mouth. "I dunno. But I had a bag with my lunch today. Mr. Kellerman had one too, so . . ."

I actually laugh. She wipes her fingertips and goes

back to the shirt. I've almost finished the bag when she holds it up.

"Ta-da!"

It's pretty amazing. You can't tell the collar was ever torn off. It may be a little stretched out, but it's better than I could have imagined.

"Thank you." I go to grab the shirt and she pulls back.

"Uh, no. Go wash your hands first, smart guy."

I do and she goes to her desk and hands me a small black comb.

I take it, but I'm wondering if it's . . . used. Yuck.

"Always be prepared. That's the School Nurse Motto. I've got an entire CVS in that desk."

I turn the comb over, unsure. I must make a face.

"It's clean. Brand-new. Zero cooties." She smiles. "But you do have a spot of ketchup on the back of your ear-lobe." She grabs a paper towel from the wall dispenser, wets it in the sink, and wipes it off.

"Be honest with me, did you get mugged by a hot dog or something?"

12.5

THE BEAST WITHIN

"How's the tapping, Andrew?" Dr. Cain had her hands clasped on her knee. It was my third visit with her.

"I . . . I mean, I'm still doing it, so. . ."

"Okay. When do you do it?"

I scratched my ear. "All the time."

She smiled. "But are there times when you do it more?"

I sat and thought about that a while. "I think I do it more when I'm mad. Or annoyed. I don't know."

"Can you give me a specific example? Maybe since the last time I saw you?"

"Yeah. A few nights ago. G . . ." I sighed, 'cause I wasn't proud of it. "She just knocked over her bottle of Coke. All over my math homework. It just . . . I knew it was gonna be sticky and get all wrinkly and smell weird and I overreacted. And then she said she hadn't done it—that I had—and that got me . . ."

Dr. Cain looked up. "Real mad?"

"I got furious." I felt my face turning red as I relived it. "I started yelling at her—like, really . . . Then finally I stopped myself and went in my room. Sat on the edge of the bed. And I tapped. I tapped a lot. I wanted to cry, but I just closed my eyes and put my head down and . . . I guess I was doing it to stop being angry? I have no idea."

"Hmm." Dr. Cain was watching me, thinking. "Maybe."

"Maybe?"

"Yeah." She leaned forward, elbows on her knees. "Usually, we don't think of anger as the thing that triggers things like tapping."

"I don't know. Maybe not." I sighed. "Maybe being angry makes me anxious—and *then* I tap?"

She nodded a few times, and I swear she had that twinkle in her eye like when a teacher sees you start to understand a math problem. "That's a thought. Does that feel right?"

"I dunno." I took a deep breath and laid my head back, closed my eyes. "Sometimes it's like he's in there, trying to get out." It came out before I thought about it.

Dr. Cain tipped her head to the side. "Who?"

"What?"

"Who's in there?"

I sat there for a long time looking at the carpet. "My Dad. Dan. I don't refer to him as Dad anymore." I turned to look out the window. A woman in a yellow dress was cleaning the window across the street from the inside. My face felt warm.

Dr. Cain went on. "So, you don't want to be angry and it makes you anxious? And the loss of control makes you anxious. That sound right?"

I nodded a few times and dropped my head back against the cushion, eyes closed. "Like an Anger Werewolf."

Dr. Cain tapped her knee with her pen. "I like that, actually." She nodded again. "It's a good visual."

Dr. Cain made a couple of quick notes. "Think about this, Andrew. Do you think you're more scared of losing control and being angry . . . or of being angry *like your dad.*"

That one landed hard enough that I felt the ground tilt a little. Was I actually a Dan Yaeger Werewolf?

I let out a long breath and sank down in the chair. Closed my eyes tight.

"Are you okay, Andrew?"

"Yep. Just . . . feeling that one."

She let me sit there for a few minutes. "Do you want to tell me a bit more about your dad? Sorry. I mean about Dan?"

"Fastidious Dan? That's what G started calling him. He's a jerk."

She wasn't letting me off that easy. "Anything more . . . specific?"

"He's gone. Way gone. West Coast gone." I scootched back up in the chair. "He doesn't help us or call me or have me out or anything." I ran a hand through my hair. "And he could. My mom says he has a decent job. But he never even answered calls. Or emails or texts or anything. I haven't gotten a birthday card since I was eight. Not that I'd even want one from him now."

"I'm sorry, Andrew. That's so hard." Her face looked sad as she wrote something down. She took a long, deep breath. "And you remember him being angry a lot?"

"Really angry." I looked around the office. I felt squirmy when I said the next part. "And, like, fussy. G said he was a clean freak. Hence the Fastidious Dan nickname. My mom said he was born with a bottle of Fantastik in his hand, and my mom and G are—well, they're messy. They just are. So he was all freaked out about things being perfect and clean and in order. And he'd lose it when they weren't. Like, really lose it. He'd take it out on my mom and me and G. Even Jonesy remembers him screaming at us about some pizza sauce on the counter."

Dr. Cain just nodded, and now I was irritated.

"I know, I know. I get it. I see it. I'm a clean freak too, and I'm tall and skinny like him and I'm fussy and a neat freak and I'm angry. Fastidious Andrew. He probably tapped and reclosed doors like me too, for all I know and it's not fair!" I stood up, a first for our sessions. I walked—stormed?—over to the bookshelf in the corner and then came back. Sat down.

"I don't want to turn into him!"

When I'd walked over to the bookshelf, I'd seen one book that was pulled out further than the rest—the spine of it was sticking out maybe an eighth of an inch over the edge of the shelf—and I wasn't gonna be able to help myself. I hated myself for it, but that voice in my head said I had to fix that book, or the world would explode or something.

Every cell in my brain was yelling this at me. So, I stood up, went over, and pushed it in. The voice quieted. I came back and sat down, arms crossed. Then I pointed at the bookshelf.

"AND YEAH I HAD TO DO THAT OR THE FRIGGIN' WORLD WAS GONNA END! SORRY! SAME AS THAT CRUMB UNDER THE PICTURE THAT TIME!" I lowered my voice a bit and said what I had to. "And . . . there's a big, long hair hanging off the bottom of your right sock too. I've been trying not to say anything, but . . ."

"Whoops!" She grabbed the hair and dropped it in the little trash can beside her chair. "Sorry. There are little no-slip nubbies on these and sometimes they act like a Swiffer."

I flopped back in the chair, annoyed at the world and my dad and life and everything, but Dr. Cain just sat there giving me one of the calmest, most infuriatingly understanding smiles of all time.

"Can I give you one more exercise—for when things get on top of you? The anger or the anxiety or, y'know, crooked books or hairy socks?"

I nodded. "Sure. Why not?"

She sat up straight in her chair and put both socked feet flat on the carpet. "Okay. This one is called visualization. But let's start with some simple breathing again.

It all comes back to breathing. You can choose to close your eyes—or look out at the sky, or up at the ceiling. However you're comfortable."

I closed my eyes, and she went on. "Okay. This is even simpler than the box breathing. Just take a deep breath and let it out really slow."

I did. I pulled in a breath and let it out as slow as I could. It was hard to go that slow, so I had to concentrate. The breath out was kind of shaky.

"Okay, try that a few more times, until it starts to feel more natural."

I sat there breathing, trying not to be self-conscious. It got easier and less shaky after a few goes.

It helped. It gave me something else to focus on than the garbage running around in my upset head.

Finally, she must have thought I was in the groove.

"Okay, Andrew. Keep breathing like that, but now I want you to think of your happiest place on earth. Like, a specific place and time. Somewhere where you're completely content. Totally happy. It could be in a park you go to, or in a movie theater before the movie starts. Take a second and think of that place. Let your mind drift there, but keep breathing."

It took me about two seconds. "Jonesy's pool. In her yard, in the summer."

Dr. Cain sounded pleased. "Oh, that's perfect." I imagined her toes wiggling happily in her colorful socks. "Now I want you to picture a perfect moment there. Really put yourself there and tell me the scene."

I thought for a second. "Jonesy and I are sitting on the edge with our feet in the water."

Dr. Cain went on. "Great. Now tell me details. Is the water cold? Warm?"

"Warm." I sort of smiled. "Her parents keep it really warm. My mom kids Mika that they have that warm pool money.'"

"Okay, great. Your feet are in the warm pool. Now tell me what you hear. What you smell. Get as specific as you can."

I took a second to really be there. "I can hear my mom and Mika laughing at the table on the deck. I can hear burgers sizzling on the grill while her dad is being Master Griller. I can smell them too."

I sensed that Dr. Cain had leaned forward. "That sounds amazing. Any more details?"

"Freshly cut grass. Mr. Jones is a nut about his yard. It's that nice soft grass you can run around in barefoot and not worry you're gonna step on anything sharp—unlike the grass around our apartments. He literally gets every stick."

"Anything more?"

"Yeah, Jonesy and I are laughing. She probably just told some dumb joke. She loves dad jokes. And we have Diet Dr Peppers. They always have those stocked."

"All right, Andrew. Now just take a few long breaths and really *be* there. Smell the grass. Taste the Dr Pepper. Feel the water on your feet and legs."

I did. I sat there for maybe a minute, picturing it. Smelling and hearing and experiencing it. Not to sound like a dork, but it was . . . really nice.

Finally, Dr. Cain told me to bring my mind back into the office. I did, opening my eyes, and she was smiling that warm smile again. "Do you feel calmer?"

I took another deep breath. "I do, kind of."

"Right? That's visualization. You can do it anytime. If you start to feel stressed or overwhelmed, you can always just . . . 'Go to the Pool.' And the more you do it, the easier it gets. The better you'll get. Try to imagine more and more specific details. Are there floats in the pool? Can you hear the bubbles in the Dr Pepper?"

"What if I'm in class, or somewhere where I can't sit back and get comfortable?"

She smiled. "The more you practice it, the better you'll get at it. You'll be able to just go there in your mind. Eyes wide open. Will you start practicing it for me?"

"I will." I sniffed. "I'll practice."

She leaned back and smiled like she was proud of me. I had been a good pupil.

"Listen, Andrew. You're gonna be okay. This is all really important stuff. This is good. We're just starting to unravel it, but you're gonna be okay. You're a good kid. We're just gonna keep working on this, and figuring out some ways to help you cope a little better, and you, young man . . ." She pointed at me. "You are gonna be fine."

I nodded, looking at my hands.

She pressed. "Do you believe me?"

I nodded again. "Yeah. Maybe we get an exorcist to get the Dan out of me."

Not to be a total bummer, but that was our last visit. Maybe I can see her more if my mom's new job works out. We'll see.

OVERWHELMED
BREEEATHE.
AM I LOSING IT? WILL I FIND IT AGAIN?
WORRY.
I HAVE TO TAP. DON'T WANNA. GOTTA.
MY SHOULDERS HURT.
TENSE.
IS THIS CHAIR STICKY?
TAP TAP
WHAT IF I DIG A HOLE AND LIVE IN IT?
I MAY BARF.
UGH.
BLEH.
WHERE IS G?
THE NOGGIN FERRETS ARE HUNGRY TODAY.
SIGH
GENE THE MEAN IS KEEN TO KICK MY SPLEEN.

13

THE LAB AND THE SQUIRREL

Mr. Stanley - Science

Walking into science class, I'm so lost in thought about G that I almost run right into Gene the Mean.

"Nice shirt, Shoestain." He's intentionally blocking my way, arms crossed, looking up at me defiantly. "What'd you do, run to the Dollar Store for a replacement?"

This isn't the first time Gene has made comments

about my clothes. It's one of his go-to jerk moves. I wonder where he gets his ideas.

Until today, I've largely managed to avoid him a lot in our time in school together—especially since his dramatic, post-third-grade Vader-like turn to the dark side—but one thing has always amused him: my knock-off, off-brand, grass-stained (from my lawn mowing jobs) sneakers. They're green—despite my best cleaning efforts—and they're like catnip for him. They're always worthy of a comment.

He's called me a variety of things in the past: Thrift Shop, Dollar Store, Walmart, Mr. Green Shoes, and his favorite—Shoestain. It's infuriating given that he always has the newest, most expensive limited-edition sought-after sneakers a kid could dream of.

I go to walk around Gene, but he steps into me. "I was talking to you, Garage Sale." I forgot. That's one too.

I stop and look down at this horrible human. My brain circuits must be absolutely fried at this point, because I break my Number One Rule—to never respond.

"They haven't kicked you out of school yet, Eugene?"

Gene's eyes blink and widen a bit in surprise and anger. He somewhat famously pounded Seth Filler's face in fifth grade when Seth made the discovery of Gene's full name. I don't think anyone has said it out loud since.

"Are you . . . ?" The look of fury that rolls across his face is like watching a hand ball into a fist. "I'm gonna—" He pushes me, but I do my best not to move. I'm taller and heavier anyway—and I've had enough.

"Oh, you're tough now? Is that it?" Gene's face is red and going to purple. "Did your daddy buy you the new shirt, or—OH, THAT'S RIGHT! Your dad isn't around, is he?"

This lands harder than a punch. Way harder. I feel

like he knocked the wind out of me. Kids have stopped. They're staring.

But Gene isn't done. "Your dad worked for my dad at one point. You know that, right?"

I do know that. I'm frozen. I'm just still, glaring back. My jaw is quivering, but it's a small quiver. Hopefully no one else can see it.

"Said there was always something off about him." Then Gene looks up like he's searching his mind. "What was it he called him?" Then he gets a big happy grin. "Oh yeah! *Dirtbag*." Gene puts his hands on his hips and smiles up at me with the nastiest smile ever. "That's it. That's the word he used. Said your dad was a gigantic dirtbag."

I'm fully shaking now. And I feel that stupid anger I inherited from my (dirtbag) dad boiling up my spine and I want to throttle Gene, but I also feel like if I move, I'll start crying. Tears are piling up behind my eyes so hard, I blink and look away.

To Gene, this is a victory. "Sounds like he used to like a drink or two. Big hothead too."

Why? Seriously, I'm asking. Why would somebody be like this? I'm back up two degrees, but it's anxiety all mixed together with anger, which is confusing.

I will not lose control. I can't get my feet to move, so I

start repeating this in my head. I will not lose control. I will not—

That's when I feel an arm land around my shoulders, pulling me toward the classroom door.

"ANFREW!! Let's not be late, partner!" It's Kendrick, and not a moment too soon. I'm not even sure he knows he's pulled me out of a situation—it may just be Kendrick being Kendrick. Inside the door, he grabs me by both shoulders as we walk back to our lab table, whisper-talking to me.

"First off, I don't know what that was back there, but it couldn't have been good. More importantly, I want to apologize again for the rocket incident. Seriously. That was an accident, but it was *my* accident and it got on you and that isn't cool at all. I'm sorry, okay? Truly."

I set my books down at our table and sit on one of the metal stools as he grabs the other. "It's . . ." I'm in shock. The ketchup in the hair is so far in the past I'm not even sure what he's talking about, at first. "It's fine." I swallow. "It's fine."

Kendrick grins and nods. "Okay. Good. But were you able to observe the sheer awesomeness of the rocket before it—you know—got you?"

I'm still shaking. "Sure."

The bell rings. Kendrick is looking over my shoulder. "Okay. Now. I seriously don't know what's up with you and Gene the Shmean, but he's grinning at you like he ate your lunch."

I can't help but turn, and sure enough, Gene is one table up and one over giving me a look like he isn't close to done. My shoulders clench and my popcorn kernel twitches as the anxiety level goes just a bit higher.

I look back at Kendrick. "Yeah, he may murder me."

"Why?"

I shrug. "Because I wouldn't help him cheat in math? I guess? Because he got in trouble?" I'm honestly not sure what the core issue is. "Because he's chosen to be pure evil?"

Kendrick grimaces. "Yeah." He nods a bit. "That's unfortunate." He goes to pull his textbook out of his backpack but looks back up at me.

"You smell like hand sanitizer."

Mr. Stanley claps his large hands at the front of the class. He's a tall, imposing teacher, but everybody likes him. He's fairly cool and even funny somctimes.

I mean, "teacher funny," but that's better than nothing.

"People. Students. Hello, hello, hello. Let's all quiet down, shall we?" The murmuring in the class drops off.

"So, first off, I heard from Mr. Abrams there was some excitement in the cafeteria today. Someone doing a little extracurricular science experiment, sounds like. Anyone in here want to take credit for that? It seems like it was a success in some ways."

The response is a whole room full of kids looking at their desks, or out the window, or anywhere but up front. This feels like a trap.

Mr. Stanley smiles and laughs.

"What if I say I'll give you extra credit?" He looks around the room, his eyes stopping on Kendrick for a second. "No? All right, suit yourselves." He shrugs and flips his textbook open to a page marked with a green Post-it note.

Mrs. Dithers comes over the intercom and calls for two more homeroom classes to come for their photos. Still not mine. I wish they'd have let us know the order, but whatever.

"Okay. I'm calling an audible today. We were going to do a different experiment, but I thought maybe we'd lean into the science of today's Ketchup Rocket. We're going to do something similar—different chemicals, but it'll explain some of the things you saw over your tater tots—but in a *much* more controlled manner. No ketchup on the ceiling in here."

Elizabeth Brunch, she of the straight A's and enormous

glasses, raises her hand from her front row center seat. "Mentos and Coke?"

Mr. Stanley pulls out a rack of test tubes. "No, but . . . While those reactions can be cool—as seen on the Tik-Tiks and the TweetTubes—we're going to use different materials so we can control it more. And analyze it."

Elizabeth, in an uncharacteristic move, slumps back in her chair with a disappointed "Aw."

"I know, I know." Mr. Stanley starts carefully pouring exact amounts of clear liquid from a large white bottle into each tube. "Now. While I set some of this up, let's talk about carbon dioxide, huh? Carbon dioxide's fun."

I'll admit it. I tune out. I can't believe I haven't heard back from Mika yet. I keep waiting for the intercom above the door to crackle to life and tell me I have a call or something. I look that way and oops, there's Gene, doing his best impression of a fixated hyena or grizzly or something. A chill races over me and now the Anxiety Follies are back in action once again.

I look away, and casually start five-tapping on the side of my metal stool, softly enough to not make a noise. (This is honestly part of the reason I chose the back row, so nobody behind me can see my taps. You think about these things when you tap.)

Looking out the window, I see a squirrel sitting on a branch gnawing away at some kind of nut. Something about how calm it looks makes me realize how keyed up I am. (*Keyed up* is a phrase I got from my mom. I think it just means freaked out.)

That squirrel looks like it doesn't have a care in the world, and I really want to go out there and join it. Seriously. Maybe I could get a squirrel costume.

That stupid squirrel is so chilled out and I feel like I can't breathe, and I have nervous electricity running in my veins and I'm so jealous of that little tree rodent that I want to scream. Is that weird? Being jealous of a squirrel?

I'm pretty sure that's weird, but there you go.

I straighten my pencil, my folder, and my book so they're all perfectly lined up with even spaces between each item. I feel like I have to—it's like the finger tapping. I do it at home with toothpaste and hairbrushes and everything on the bathroom sink. And the kitchen counter. And my dresser. I've had to get out of bed sometimes to make sure things in the kitchen were evenly spaced enough.

It shuts that little voice up, but it's a pain. It's exhausting. It's constant.

I close my eyes and start my counting/breathing, but that's when Mr. Stanley comes by and puts a test tube in Kendrick's and my holder.

He also gives each table a little dish with some tiny crystals on it—almost like salt grains—and the tiniest little spoon I've ever seen. He's talking, and explaining everything, but the nerves in my head are buzzing so loud, I don't hear anything. I just nod wisely when he looks at me.

The lesson continues for a while, but I'm in the clouds. My chest feels three sizes too small, and every time I try to listen, I picture G in a ditch—or Jonesy's hurt face—or Gene knocking my face clean off my head or Jonesy never hanging out with me again, or my mom looking completely horrified when she opens my pack of school photos.

Finally—I have no idea how much time has passed—I hear Mr. Stanley emphasizing a point. Really driving it home. Something about his tone breaks through my fog.

"I'm not kidding. Two crystals in your measuring spoon. Not three. Not four. I know that seems like nothing, but trust me, I'll know if you do more. This is a *controlled experiment*, okay? So get two crystals in your spoon now."

I grab the spoon and carefully place two crystals into it. Then Kendrick reaches over and drops a few more in, giving me a big, charming Kendrick smile, eyebrows raised. I shoot him the most deadpan look I have in me and dump them all back out. I carefully put two back in. Kendrick shrugs and laughs with a "had to try" look.

Mr. Stanley is back at the front of the room. "Okay. Now, in an orderly fashion, I'm going to have you go get aprons and goggles from the hooks before we do this. No joking around, okay? Let's remember all the safety protocols we've—"

Just then the intercom over the door crackles again and lets out a squawk. My heart jumps—this is it! They found G! They already called homerooms, so this has to be about her!

It's Principal Espinosa, long-winded as always. Just get to it!

"I need Kendrick Stevens to report immediately to the principal's office, posthaste. Please give Kendrick a hall pass and direct him this way. Thank you, and pardon the interruption."

My heart sinks as Kendrick leans back on his stool. "Gah!! Somebody ratted!" Several people in the class laugh and somebody says "Oops" in a cartoony voice. I feel bad that he's being called down there, but worse that this wasn't the "All Clear on G" announcement I'd hoped for.

Mr. Stanley has his arms crossed, smiling. "Mister

Stevens. I had my suspicions. It seems you're better at science than you let on in here."

Kendrick is cramming his folder down into his pack. "I have no idea what you're talking about, Mr. S. This is a clear case of mistaken identity." But he's kind of smiling. He's been to the principal's so often, he probably has a chair with his name on it in there.

I watch as Kendrick throws his backpack over one shoulder and walks up the aisle while Mr. Stanley digs around in his desk drawer for the hall pass. He holds it out to Kendrick.

"Just an idea, but if you can explain the science behind the Ketchup Rocket, maybe Espinosa'll go easy on you."

Kendrick grabs it, shaking his head. "Yeah, but where's the fun in that?"

Just then I sense motion to my right and look over. Gene is scurrying back from my table to his. He's taken advantage of Mr. Stanley being distracted again, but what did he do?

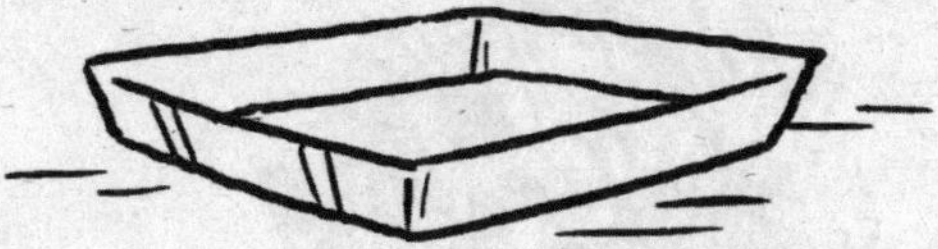

I notice my little dish of crystals is empty and panic.

Now . . . here's where you have the advantage, reading about this. For example, I'm sure you would know at this point not to look down into the test tube to see if Gene dumped the crystals in there. You've probably caught on that this is a day that CAN and WILL get worse. All I can say is that my brain is out to lunch or something. I act without thinking.

Once again, time slows down. I put my hands on the lab table and lean over to look in, just as whatever chemical reaction Mr. Stanley has concocted causes the contents to change color and geyser up like a cannon blast of dark purple foam. I see it coming—I'm looking straight down the barrel after all—but fast reflexes clearly aren't my thing.

The only sound from the reaction is a cartoonish *FWOOOOMP,* which makes things a little more surreal. I manage to keep my mouth closed this time, but hear a strangled grunt come out of my nose anyway. As I stumble back, I hear Mr. Stanley call out my name.

I clamp my eyes shut as tight as I can—again, I have NOT been paying attention, so I have zero idea what's all over me. I hear people scrambling around, some gasps, and teacher-shoed feet running to me, but also the unmistakable sound of Gene the Mean laughing.

No, not just laughing.

Braying.

I read that description in a book once—I think it's

the sound a donkey makes when it's all excited. And as my butt hits the counter at the back of the room—and I slide to the ground, and I feel Mr. Stanley's gigantic hands on my shoulders and hear him telling me to keep my eyes closed—that's the image I have in my mind: Gene the Mean braying his big stupid head off so hard, he has to clutch his sides to keep from exploding in delight.

14

SAFETY PROTOCOLS

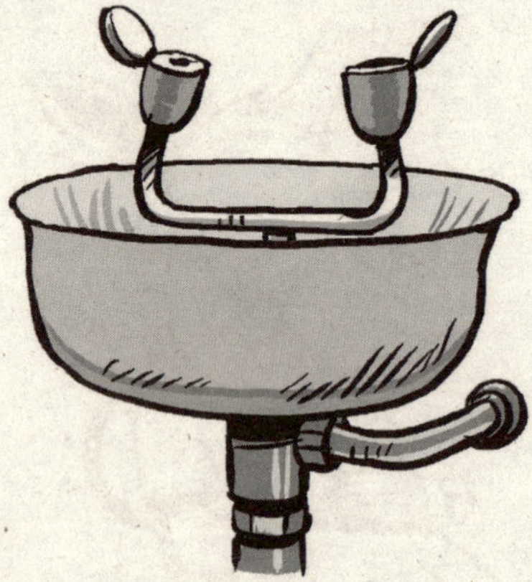

Mr. Stanley sounds calm, but what he says freaks me out a little.

"Andrew, let's get you to the eye wash station, okay?" He takes one of my elbows and helps me to my feet.

This, and the way the class immediately goes quiet, sends me into what G would call a "tizzy". I'm edging closer to that last notch on the Kernel Scale.

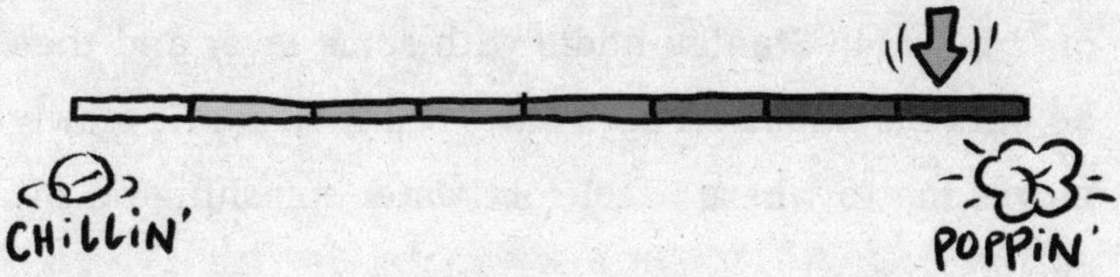

We went over the safety stuff at the beginning of the year—the eye station, the shower with the pull cord in the corner—but those always seemed like they were for some bizarre, never-gonna-happen emergency. Like, I remember even wondering if the shower was hooked up. We're only doing seventh-grade experiments, after all. But now here I am with my eyes clamped shut, headed for that weird attachment on the corner sink. Am I gonna go blind? Are the chemicals gonna burn the eyeballs out of my skull??

"You're fine, Andrew. It's nothing that's gonna do anything to you, but let's just . . . be sure." Again, this doesn't slow my racing heart. We stop and I hear the water turn on. I hear Mr. Stanley fiddle with some lever and then he puts his hands on both sides of my head. He slowly moves me to where I feel cold water splashing on my eyelids.

"Okay, I know it's weird, but just . . . open your eyes. Let the water rinse them out."

Opening my eyes is the last thing I want to do. "Is it gonna hurt?"

"I . . ." Mr. Stanley sounds flustered. "I don't think so? I've gotta be honest, I've never had to use the eye wash station in twelve years of teaching."

AUTHOR'S NOTE:
SO NOT HELPING.

I feel his hands holding my head steady, and slowly open my eyes. (Or I at least try to open the swollen one.) It doesn't hurt but it doesn't exactly feel good, either. After a few seconds, Mr. Stanley's grip on my head eases up.

"Okay. You okay? Feel like they got rinsed?"

I close my eyes tight again. "I think so." My nose is running too. Someone grabs my arm and puts some paper towels in my hand. I wipe at my whole face.

"Let me see." Mr. Stanley turns me around.

I blink a bit and it seems okay. He's a few inches from

my nose, his hand on my shoulder. "There you go. You okay, buddy?"

I look around—the entire class is staring at me. Elizabeth of the big glasses is actually wringing her hands. Another kid, Amir Patel, has his hand on his chest like he'd be clutching his pearls if he was wearing some.

And there's Gene in the back, a smirk on his face. I look at Mr. Stanley. "I'm okay. I'm fine."

A look of relief comes over my teacher. "Okay. I thought so, but . . . it really got you. Best not to take any chances." He looks around. "Everybody back to your seats. Show's over."

Kendrick is standing there with the wooden pass still in his hand. "Your shirt is, um . . ."

I look down and my shirt looks like a tie-dye. Dark purple splotches cover most of it. Then I realize there are purple splotches on my arms too. I look up at Kendrick.

He winces. "Your face too. Like you got in a fight with a grape Slush-O."

Mr. Stanley snaps his fingers. "Kendrick. Get to the office." He points at the door. "Gonna get *me* in trouble if you don't hurry."

Kendrick laughs, but hesitates. I think he's waiting to see if I'm okay. Amir pipes up.

"Dude. I hope you didn't, like . . . like that shirt." I feel my heart sink a bit. My inner popcorn kernel twitches.

Mr. Stanley has his hands on his hips now, looking me up and down. "What did you do? Put all the crystals in there?"

I start to protest, but before I can say anything, Kendrick jumps in. "No way. I wanted to put in more, and he stopped me."

Mr. Stanley makes a face at Kendrick. "Of course you did. So then, who did it?"

He looks around the room. I'm aware of the absolute silence in the room—nobody wants to snitch on Gene.

I might, but something is happening. In my brain, I think. I'm staring at the floor and I realize I'm starting to shake. I plop back onto my metal stool, which clangs and slides. I feel like energy is coursing through my arms and chest. Through my muscles and blood. I'm thinking I know what a robot must feel like when its circuits get too much juice.

Oh, no. No, no, no.

I've felt this before, and I'd really hoped I never would again.

A panic attack.

I can NOT let this happen here. I have to keep myself in control.

I tap the underside of the table and start doing my box breathing. Be a Navy SEAL, Andrew. Be a Navy SEAL. No panic. No panic.

"Andrew? You okay?"

I look up at Mr. Stanley's face and the edges of my vision are dimming. I'm starting to panic about not panicking.

"I'm not sure."

"Oh, boy." Mr. Stanley hops past me and grabs a glass beaker thing from the back shelf. He fills it with water and hands it to me, his hand on my back. "Drink this."

I look at the glass and wonder how many weird

chemicals and experiments have been in there—the germ thing never lets up—but the water does look good. I drink it in one go and it tastes okay.

"I'm gonna send you down to the nurse's office, okay?"

I lower my head, nodding. This has got to be a single-day-nurse-visit record. Nurse Finnegan is gonna think I'm stalking her. But if I'm going to flip my lid, I'd rather it happen there than here in class.

I stand up and test my legs. Wobbly, but they seem stable enough. At least for standing.

"Kendrick has my only hall pass, but just go ahead. If anyone stops you, tell them you have my permission."

Numb and buzzing, I nod and walk for the door. I'm not moving fast. I'm a zombie. But I do hear Gene let out a nasal grunt of a laugh as I go by him.

As I pass into the hall, I feel like parts of me are shutting down. Maybe it's a protective thing your brain does? It occurs to me that maybe every anxiety attack is different, like snowflakes.

I'm slogging past the math room when Mr. Harris steps out to shut his door. He stops cold when he sees me.

"Andrew? Are you all right?" He looks genuinely concerned, so I must look like I was in an explosion. I mean . . . I was.

I nod and keep going.

"You sure?"

He's behind me now, and I don't trust my voice to not break or squawk, so I just raise a purple-stained thumbs-up.

I get maybe twenty more feet down the hall before the intercom system comes back to life. I stop.

"Andrew Yaeger and Aisha Jones, report to the principal's office. Thank you." It's Principal Espinosa's voice, but he sounds so blunt. So not how he talks that my heart starts racing. Either they have G or there's bad news.

A lump the size of a Cadbury Egg forms in my throat as I take off running for the front office, my wobbly legs completely forgotten.

FUN NICKNAMES FOR ANXIETY!
THE BUZZIES
STEAMBRAIN
egg
SSSSSSS
SIZZLEMELON
HISS
CHITTER
NOGGIN FERRETS

15

THE FUZZ

Flying through the office door, I'm shocked to see two police officers in full uniform standing there talking with Principal Espinosa and Mrs. Dithers. All four of them turn, and their eyes open wide.

"What the what?" It pops out of the principal's mouth. Mrs. Dithers says my name and actually makes the sign of the cross over her chest.

One of the officers steps forward. "Are you okay, son? What happened to your face?"

I try to shake off the question. "Nothing. Science. Is my grandma okay?"

The other officer, a female—older than my mom but shorter than me by several inches—steps up. "Actually, that's what we're here about, Andrew." She looks concerned.

Now that she's moved out of the way, I see Kendrick sitting on a chair in Espinosa's office. He leans way over and gives me a smile, eyebrows raised. The mostly empty ketchup bottle is sitting on a towel on the principal's desk.

The door slams open behind me and Jonesy rushes in.

"What's happening? Did they find her?" She's out of breath. Then she sees me and stops cold. Her eyes don't even go wide—it's like she has no way to process how I look. I'm sure she's still irritated with me too, so that makes it extra weird.

"Well . . ." The female officer puts her hands on her hips. "No. That's why we're here. You're Aisha?"

Jonesy nods and the officer goes on.

"Your mom thought one—or both of you—might have some new ideas?" She gives us both a sad, hopeful smile.

If my head was on fire before, this turns me into a full-body forest fire. They don't know what to do so they're asking *US*? Kids?? I feel like I might black out, and then I notice Jonesy's hand on my shoulder. She may still be mad, but she's there.

I start in. "You checked the Donut Den, right? McDonald's? By the dumpster?"

Both cops are nodding, their mouths in tight lines.

"Ditches? Did you check ditches?? Watery ditches??" I know this sounds nuts as I say it, but it comes out anyway.

They both give me a confused look. "We've been looking everywhere we could think of."

I run a half-purple hand through my hair. "Okay. Okay. Has Mika tried my mom's phone again?"

"She has. Over and over." The male cop sits down in a chair like he's trying to come down to my level. "So, Aisha's mom is—understandably—in a bit of a state. We wanted to contact your mom's new employer. At first, she just didn't want to worry your mom on her big day, but now she . . ." He winces. "She can't remember your mom's new boss's name."

Jonesy tips her head back, exasperated. "Guh. Mo-o-m!"

I've got this, I think. "It's Mister Mc . . . Mc . . ." Oh no. I keep wanting to say McAlister's, but that's the deli over off Third Street. (Good, but not nearly as good as Dagwood's Sub Shop.)

How can I not know this? I feel like G, having one of her word blocks. Panic isn't making it any easier. "McSomething??"

Jonesy gives me a look. "Seriously?" But then she sees the helplessness on my face and follows it with a quick "Sorry" and a shoulder squeeze.

I feel like my brain has frozen. Like it's gone "toes up," as G used to say. I've heard my mom say the name a hundred times and . . . was I not listening? Am I already turning into a jerky teenager who never listens? I'm not even thirteen yet! I feel a wash of guilt come over me before something tickles my brain.

"Oh! Oh, wait!"

Everyone freezes. "His business card! My mom . . ."

I remember after she had her second interview with the guy—when she was pretty sure she was going to get the job—she came home with a stack of business cards. I was doing homework at the dining room table and G was (loudly) crunching through a French bread pizza. Well, I was supposed to be doing my homework, but I'd really been trying to draw Garfield from memory. It hadn't gone well.

Mom slid a card across the table to me. "Put this somewhere you won't lose it," and I put it . . . somewhere??

Basically, I'd lost it.

"I have his business card. It's either . . . in a folder or one of my textbooks. No, wait. It was a workbook. English! My English notebook!" I turn to the principal and point over my shoulder. "My locker?"

"Go!" He says it with an urgency that matches mine. It might be the shortest thing he's ever said.

I sprint off as fast as I can, and realize Jonesy is right beside me. Okay, she's faster, so not *right* beside me. She gets to my locker first. As I'm spinning my combo lock, I mutter, "J, I'm sorry about earlier."

She bounces on her toes, ready to go. "No worries. We'll talk later. Get that card!"

Two minutes and twenty-three seconds later, we're back in the office, out of breath, but with my workbook and Don McAndrews's business card. McAndrews! I'd tucked it into a soul-crushingly boring lesson on diagramming sentences.

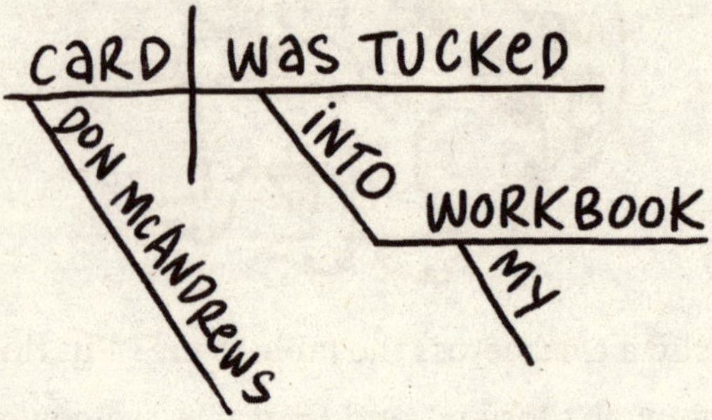

I hand it to the female officer and she—Martinez, according to her name tag—pulls out her iPhone. She dials and we all wait anxiously while the phone rings on speaker. I see that even Kendrick, elbows on his knees, is watching and chewing at a fingernail.

One ring. Two.

And then I hear my mom's voice from the cell phone, all business-like:

"Don McAndrews's office. How may I help you?"

My reaction is crazy. I feel warmth rush through my body, but tears spring into my eyes, making everything go wavy. It's just her voice, but . . . I guess I really, really needed to hear it.

Officer Martinez sounds relieved as well. "Oh, thank goodness. Is this Susan Yaeger?"

She sounds caught off guard. "It is."

Officer Martinez lays out the situation in the fewest, kindest words possible, giving my mom time to ask a handful of frantic questions. When she hears the school mentioned, my mom's tone changes. "Wait. You're at the school?"

"Hi, Mom," I chime in. "I'm here."

My mom's voice catches in her throat. "Oh, honey. Are . . . are you okay?"

Now, *that's* a loaded question, I think, and I almost laugh. I'm looking down—through my one working eye—at the dark purple stains on my shirt and arms. "I'm fine, Mom. Just worried about G."

"I know you are, Andrew, I am too. I'm . . . I'm heading home now." She sounds hesitant.

Jonesy winces. She whispers to Officer Martinez, "She's worried she'll lose this job. First day."

Martinez looks back to the phone. "Okay. Mrs. Yaeger, could you do me a favor and let me talk with your employer? Mr. McAndrews, is it?"

My mom sniffs. "Yeah. Yes. I see him coming down the hall."

The officer goes on. "Great. In the meantime, I'm

sending Andrew and Aisha back to class. Officer Davis and I will meet you at your house. Ms. Jones is there as well."

I'm shaking my head. "Nope. No. I'm coming with you."

Officer Davis shakes his head and walks us to the office door. "No way. School wins. Always. We've got this, and now your mom is on the case. The cavalry is on its way, as they say."

I have no idea what that means or who says it. My mind is racing. The bell rings as he steps out into the hall with us.

He smiles at us both. "Ya done good. Seriously. Try to relax."

I'm watching kids pour out of the band room across the hall, thinking that relaxing must be easier for other people. They sure throw that word around a lot.

Officer Davis looks down the hall for a moment. "Does Harris still teach math here?"

I nod. "Yeah. I had him this morning."

Officer Davis smiles. "He was a tough one. But I liked him, y'know?"

Jonesy and I stare at him before she bumps my arm. "Okay. Art class? Nurse?"

I want to run in eight directions and throw things and scream and take a nap and pull my hair out all at once, but I don't have those options, so I just. . . don't.

"Art."

16

ART THERAPY

Mr. Kellerman - Art

Jonesy and I walk into the art room and as she goes off to her table, I go straight to the back sink. I know Mr. Kellerman keeps some mineral spirits on the shelf underneath. That should help with what must be a nasty stain on my face, judging by people's reactions. There's also a small hand mirror hanging on the wall. (The old full mirror broke and has never been replaced.)

I turn on the water, glance up at the mirror—and freeze. It's a jolt.

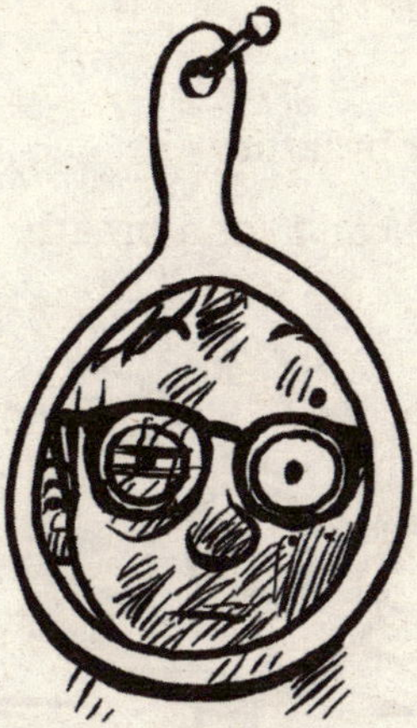

It's way worse than I'd imagined. So much worse. I'm leaning in to get a better look when I hear Mr. Kellerman's deep voice beside me.

"Good lord, A. You get into it with a squid?"

I look up at him, and I must look half out of my mind.

Maybe I am.

He goes on. "Because, you know . . . ink. Squids . . . they squirt ink."

I don't know why that glance in the tiny sink mirror is the final straw, but it is. In a day of straws, this one is the straw that puts me over the edge. The straw that pushed.

It feels dumb that the thing that tips the scale is about how I look, but it's just the awful icing on a really crappy, disgusting cake.

I feel like I can't breathe.

Like, seriously. I can't get a breath.

"Yeah, squid." I try to act normal. Maybe if I just keep going, the panic attack won't find me. Won't take me down the rabbit hole. "No. It's from . . ." Without completing my thought, I grab the bottle of mineral spirits and start fumbling with the cap. It's one of those push down and turn things and my stupid shaky fingers aren't cooperating. Finally, Mr. Kellerman takes it from my hands.

"You okay there, buddy?" He twists the cap off in one quick motion. Then he grabs a faded red rag from a cardboard box next to the sink, tips the can, and wets it. The odor is strong, but it smells like it'll do the job.

He takes my left arm in one of his huge hands and starts scrubbing at a small spot. His presence is calming, but it's way too little, way too late. I feel like things are moving super fast—like somebody hit the 2x button on my life remote.

This is happening.

Again.

At school.

I know it's happening, like I'm watching a speeding train barrel down on me.

That uncomfortable electricity and weight in my shoulders is squeezing and pushing in and threatening to drop me to my knees.

I feel . . . heavy. Like gravity has gone 2x as well. Or 3x. Or 10x.

"Andrew?" I realize Mr. Kellerman's watching me, eyebrows raised.

"Yeh?" I swallow. "Yeah?"

I want so bad to stop this—to return to normal—but it feels like the train has left the station.

I'm unraveling.

My kernel is popping.

Right here.

Right now.

Kellerman takes the rag away from my arm, and the spot looks a little better. It's still stained, but it's lighter.

I grab the rag out of his hand—I'm not trying to be rude, but I'm on autopilot. I lean into the mirror and start scrubbing at my face. The fumes sting my good eye, but I don't care.

I want this purple off of me *now.*

Now Jonesy is there too. "Careful around your eyes. Don't get any . . ."

I scrub harder. Faster. More frantically.

I think I'm trying to wipe away more than the purple. I want to wipe away the whole day.

The Missing G situation.

Gene.

The ruined shirt.

The anger.

Dan (aka Dad).

The argument with Jonesy.

The job my mom is probably gonna lose.

All of it.

I feel Mr. Kellerman's hand on my back. "Hey, hey. Slow down, A. Easy. You're gonna give yourself *another* shiner."

I dump more of the spirits on the rag and move to my arms.

Scrubbing. Grinding at them hard enough to draw blood.

I can tell I'm starting to shake. I must look out of control. No, I definitely am. I've lost it.

I can hear my breath coming in and out, louder and louder. It's *raspy* and *frantic* and the thought occurs to me I might be starting to hyperventilate. That's a new twist this time.

Do I need to breathe into a paper bag?

That's what they do in cartoons, right? I could empty out that bag of Flamin' Hot Cheetos in my backpack and breathe into it, but knowing my luck today my lungs would burst into cheese flames or something.

My breathing is out of control now, my heart is beating like a jackhammer, and I'm starting to sweat and

Here.

We.

Go.

This is a "Full-Fledged Panic Attack."

In class.

On full display.

My worst fear is happening.

Somewhere deep in my brain, I frantically try to "Go to the Pool," as Dr. Cain would call it. I squeeze my eyes shut and try to picture Jonesy and me on the edge of her pool. I try to smell the new-mown grass. I try to hear my mom and Mika and smell the burgers, but my eyes open as I realize I can't be there. Have I not practiced it enough? Did I wait too long? I think about my breathing stuff, but it feels like my lungs belong to the attack now.

My vision blurs.

Tears are on the way.

I know it sounds like I'm just throwing out a laundry list of things going wrong, but it's beyond crazy. If my body had a control panel, every single warning light would be lit up and flashing. Alarms and sirens would be sounding.

All rational thinking has stopped. The sound of blood rushing in my ears is almost all I can hear.

The best I can describe it is that my brain is a trapped badger, and all it's doing is reacting.

Which helps explain what happens next.

Mr. Kellerman tries to put his hands on my shoulders . . . and my inner cornered badger lashes out. My panicked brain sees even his attempt to calm me down as a threat . . .

. . . and I hit him.

My arm lashes out and I hit him—*hard*—across the face with the back of my wrist. It makes a sickening *POP* sound, and I know it hurts too, because his face and body react.

He winces and steps back, stunned. But immediately—even as I hear gasps from the class and someone yelps—*he's* apologizing to *me*.

"My fault! My bad! Don't grab the bear!" Whatever that means. I'm a bear?

I sink to the floor.

My legs aren't working right. All I can hear is my racing heartbeat and that whooshing in my ears.

WHOOSH WHOOSH WOOSH WOOSH

There's a flash of awareness that I just clocked my favorite teacher in the face, but it's just that. A flash in a whirlwind.

Suddenly, here are the big tears. The real ones.

They arrive, full force, as I'd always feared they would.

The whole class is watching—just like in my visions of this.

I'm mortified, but that part of me is in another state where I can't even care. In another part of the multiverse.

I'm crying and shaking and I'm still scrubbing at this arm and then the other, then back. I can barely hear Jonesy.

"Andrew? Earth to Andrew. You in there, buddy? Everything's okay."

That part breaks through the chaos. It fits. It doesn't help, but it fits. I feel like I'm being yanked out of reality . . .

The world is getting further away . . .

Losing radio contact . . .

I'm bawling now. In big, hitching sobs.

My nose is running too. Running freely. Through my blurry eye, I can see all the other students staring at me. Stunned.

Some are standing.

Some have gathered around.

A few have their hands over their mouths like they're watching a car crash. I wouldn't want to miss a show like this either.

I must be one heck of a sight, I think. The freaked-out look on their faces is too much, so I look away.

I wipe at a long strand of snot—or spit, I'm not sure which—hanging from my face.

And now my breath is coming in and out in big, loud, whooping gasps.

This is genuine, grade A panic.

Like, "waking up and the serial killer is in your room" panic. Or "watching someone you love fall off a cliff" panic.

I hear Mr. Kellerman's booming voice, loud but calm, firm but kind:

"Everyone, let's get to your seats. Sit down. Okay, Jonesy: You run and get the nurse. Tell her I'm taking Andrew outside to get some fresh air." He has one big hand on my arm, the other around my back, holding me steady. I hear Jonesy's sneakers squeak out of the classroom at full speed. "Elizabeth." (He's talking to Elizabeth—a teacher's pet in all classes.) "Elizabeth, you're in charge 'til I'm back. Everybody, listen to Elizabeth. Be a jerk and you'll answer to me. I'm talking to you, Braden."

Braden is no Gene, but he's been known to jerk it up at times.

With that, Mr. Kellerman takes the soaked rag out of my hand and tosses it in the sink. He—tentatively at first, until he knows I'm not gonna clobber him again—gets a big hand under each of my armpits and helps me to my feet, then puts his arm around me for support. It feels like I'm breathing all the air in the world—sucking it into me in big howling breaths—but I still feel like I'm suffocating.

Like there's not enough oxygen in the air.

We leave the art room—slowly—and turn right. It's actually the last room at the end of this hall, so we reach the door in no time. I hesitate.

"Alarm." (I'm a rule follower to the core.)

Kellerman pushes on through the door. "Whatever." He stops to let it close behind us.

With his help, we sit down on the top of three cement stairs. I lean forward and grab my knees and try to take a normal breath, but it keeps coming in those awful raspy whoops, and that spins me out even more.

I tip over onto my side, away from Kellerman, but I feel his hand on my arm—making sure I don't roll off the side of the stairs.

My face is on the concrete, tiny loose pebbles poking my cheek, but *I don't care*. Right on all the shoe dirt and germs and bird poop and who knows what, but I'm too far gone to care.

I close my eyes tight for a while and try to disappear.

I hear Mr. Kellerman saying "You're safe, Andrew" in his calmest voice. "I'm here. We're gonna get through this."

I can hear him, but it sounds like he's so far away.

And muffled, like the adults in a Charlie Brown special. But some of it gets through. My ears have apparently stopped working right. That's new too.

So, I just lie there, completely clenched. For I have no idea how long.

Time has kind of lost all meaning.

Like it's stopped.

Or doesn't exist.

Or it's racing by.

I have no idea.

It could have been ten minutes.

Could have been a month. Or a year.

Eventually, the uncomfortable, edgy, gnawing feeling flooding through me makes my body feel like it needs to change positions.

I sit back up.

Grab my knees again.

Rock forward and back. For a while.

My eyes are crammed shut.

Then, after who knows how long, they stay closed, but the scrunching eases a little bit.

Eventually, almost like waking up, I let them crack open, just a bit.

Looking across Second Street at the line of pine trees in front of the apartments, I try as hard as I can to slow my breathing.

It's really difficult. My heart is still racing. There's a buzzing in my ears like a squadron of drones.

I'm antsy times a million and sitting still is tough. Breathing like a normal human is almost impossible.

I lean back.

I sit forward again.

There isn't a position that helps. I squeeze my eyes shut tight again, ignoring the pain from the black eye.

Finally, I sense Mr. Kellerman shifting as he leans his considerable weight back against the door behind us.

"Okay. Let's try a thing."

I don't answer, so he waits a couple minutes before he tries again.

"Tell me five things you can see, Andrew."

I curl tighter into myself and shake my head. I'm actively dying and he wants to play games like we're two pals on a long drive?

Seriously?

WAYS TO HELP YOURSELF IN A PANIC ATTACK
BREATHE.
DIFFICULT, YET SOOTHING.
IN. OUT. REPEAT.
TOUCH SOMETHING REAL.
THANK YOU WALL, FOR BEING WALL.
SIT OR LAY DOWN AND CLOSE YOUR EYES.
DARK IS NICE.
REMIND YOURSELF A VELOCIRAPTOR ISN'T CHASING YOU.
ARE WE POSITIVE?
EVEN THOUGH IT FEELS LIKE IT.

17

STEP THERAPY

Vaguely, I know that Mr. Kellerman is trying to chill me out—but reality seems really *really* far away.

It feels like there's a skyscraper pushing into my chest and my heart is going to burst out of me and seven death metal bands are screeching at the same time inside my head.

I'm frozen.

Mr. Kellerman sits back up and bumps his elbow into me. "Seriously. Open your eyes and tell me five things you can see."

It takes me a second, but I finally grunt and lift my head.

The first thing I see is grass. "Grass." My voice sounds scratchy and *quivery*.

Like someone else's.

"Good. What else?"

My knees are right there—shaking—so: "Knees. My knees."

"That's two."

I look around a bit and a shiver runs over my entire

body, contorting me. "Shoes . . . Trees . . ." I spot part of an old Snickers wrapper in the grass about four feet out. "Wrapper."

Kellerman rubs my back. "Nice job. Now. Name me four things you can touch. And actually do it. Name them and touch them."

All right, all right.

I'm shaking like a leaf, but I think I can do this.

It seems beyond stupid, but I know he's trying to pull me back to the real world.

The "REAL WORLD." Whatever that is anymore.

"Knee." I tap it. "Top step . . . My hand . . . The railing." I touch each thing in turn.

"You're doing great, Andrew. Now: Tell me three things you can hear."

I close my eyes again. I hear a bird chirping off by the trees. "Bird." A truck goes by, rattling. "Truck . . . Music from the apartments."

"Yep. I think it's Led Zeppelin." He listens. "'Gallows Pole,' pretty sure. Now, two things you can smell."

"Grass . . . Onions, maybe?"

He laughs. "That might be my lunch. Now, one thing you can taste."

I look over at him, trying to think if there's anything. "I just taste mouth-taste. Nothing specific."

Mr. Kellerman nods and laughs. "That counts as a taste, I think." He rubs my back again. "Any better?"

I look around. I still feel panicked, but it did take a bit of the edge off. I feel like I'm back in the general vicinity of reality, at least.

"Maybe? Like ten percent?"

"Well, that's a good start. I've had panic attacks where I'd kill for ten percent."

I look back over, surprised. "You get them?"

He nods. "I do."

It's hard to imagine. Mr. Kellerman seems like the most laid-back easygoing person who ever was. He's the human version of a big St. Bernard sprawled out in a sunbeam.

"Yeah, I get 'em too. They're absolutely the worst."

We sit in silence for a bit while I process that. In my head, I name a few things I can see. Lady walking poodle. Domino's delivery car. Then my mind serves up the image of my wrist hitting Mr. K and my stomach drops.

I spin to face him. "Oh my God, I hit you! I'm so sorry!" I feel horrible. Truly. I feel like a monster.

Mr. Kellerman meets my eyes. "Andrew, listen to me. You're fine. You weren't in your head right then, okay? I came in too fast. I will never, *ever* be upset by that."

"Did it hurt?"

He laughs. "Yeah, it hurt! You've got a future in boxing. But it's fine. It wasn't you. It's forgotten."

The idea that I can just lose control makes me groan and curl into my knees again.

Mr. K takes a few loud breaths through his nose. "Just breathe. In and out. Slowly. Feel the concrete under your feet. Under your butt. That's real and everything else is just. . ." He makes a vanishing gesture with his hand. "Just breathe. We got you."

I'm not sure who he means by "we," but I just breathe.

I take my glasses off and put my face in one purple-stained hand, like my mom when she's paying bills. I try my breathing thing. In four. Hold four. Out four. Hold four. In four . . .

I five-tap on the step a few times, but it feels ridiculous in the face of what I just went through. This wasn't a wave of anxiety; this was a tidal wave of terror.

Finally, after a while, I feel my shoulders ease a bit. I lift my head and look around. Then back at Mr. Kellerman; who has his face turned up to the sun and his hands laced over his stomach.

"You really have anxiety?" I still can't believe it.

He sighs. "Yeah. Anxiety. Panic attacks. The works. I'm an old pro."

A random shiver goes through my body, making me

convulse for a second; then it's gone. "That's . . . Somehow that doesn't make me feel much better."

He smiles and sits forward. "I haven't had a panic attack in years. I've gotten way better at managing it all."

I hang my head, stretching out my neck. "Managing it. Not curing it?"

He pats my back a couple of times. "I don't think you really 'cure' anxiety. It's part of you, you know? But you'll get better at . . . coping? Living with it?"

I look up at him with what must be a blank stare, because he laughs again.

"I know that doesn't sound great. But eventually you'll start to think of it as . . ." He scratches at his beard. "Almost like an annoying friend. Your annoying, anxious, worry-wart friend who shows up at the worst times."

I'm still staring, but I think I know exactly what my anxiety pal would look like.

Mr. Kellerman stretches his legs straight out in front of him and waggles his sandaled feet. It looks funny for a big guy like him. "You'll kind of learn to expect it. Or you can sort of tell it to shut up when you need to."

He sniffs and rubs his nose. "Anxiety is actually kind of interesting, if you look at it from . . . kind of from the outside. Like . . . you're a creative kid, Andrew. I see it in class. You have an active imagination. Dreaming up ideas and cool stuff comes easy to you. But the flip side of that is that your brain is just as good at imagining bad stuff. Worst-case scenarios. I think anxiety is something that kind of goes hand in hand with being sensitive . . . imaginative . . . thoughtful. Sometimes it's just hard to keep all those great traits in line, y'know? I mean, that's just another way to think about—"

Just then, Jonesy comes hurrying around the corner of the building. I feel my shoulders release a little more.

"They're here!!" Jonesy yells this to Nurse Finnegan, who comes around the corner right behind her. She looks a little frantic, some of her hair flying around.

"We were looking around out front and by the gym."

"Sorry." Mr. Kellerman gets up to make room for Nurse F. "We took the fastest path to fresh air."

"Andrew? How are you doing?" Nurse Finnegan has

a stethoscope and an electronic blood pressure thing in her hand, but she just sits down and places the back of her hand against my cheek, which feels very nurse-y and comforting.

"I'm a *little* better. I can kind of breathe now." I look from her to Jonesy and back. "That sucked."

She laughs, but her voice is strained. "Yeah, it sounds like it did." She takes my wrist and feels for my pulse. She goes quiet for a second. "You're calming down?"

I take a couple gulps of air. "Yeah. Maybe. Slowly."

Jonesy—her arms crossed—kicks the toe of my shoe and lets out a sigh. "You about gave me a heart attack, jerk."

"Yeah." I nod a bit. "Sorry."

Jonesy sits down on the bottom step and pats my shoe. It's only then that I see she's shaking as well. She looks up at me with tears in her eyes and a quivering lip.

"That was *really* freakin' scary, Andrew! I had no idea you . . . that it could be that . . ." She waves her hand around at the whole scene, and one of the tears breaks loose, down her face, and I can't stand that I made that happen. She reaches for my hand.

I take it and squeeze. Hard. I have a lump in my

throat or else I'd thank her. I want to thank them all, from the bottom of my freak show heart. But who needs more blubbering?

I make a mental note to thank them with every stupid ounce of my being.

Later.

18

THE COMEDOWN

Mr. Kellerman's Art Room

After fussing over me a bit more, Nurse Finnegan offers to go inside and cover our class for a bit. Mr. Kellerman thanks her, and I notice that he gently grabs her wrist for a few seconds before she goes up the steps. Definitely something going on there.

As the door closes behind her, Jonesy turns. "Wait, is

there not an alarm on that door? It has that big sign and the bar thing!"

Mr. Kellerman shakes his head. "No idea."

Jonesy puts her hands on her hips and makes a face. "Well, that's not right."

I turn to Mr. Kellerman. "I can probably go back in now. I mean, I feel like I ran two or three marathons and I have a massive headache and I don't think I'll ever be this embarrassed again in my life—but I'm pretty sure I'm not going to explode or anything. I think."

Mr. K gives my knee a bump. "No . . . I think let's just sit for a bit longer. There's no rush." He looks around. "And it's nice out."

He's right about that. And I genuinely worry that when I step foot back in that room, I'll burst into embarrassment flames. Getting sprayed with an experiment in science? That was embarrassing, but it was something someone did *to* me. This one was all me. All me and my messed-up brain. And I cried like a toddler in front of *everyone*. Ugh.

The three of us sit for a while, talking. Not about panic attacks. About dumb stuff. The latest Marvel movie: Mr. Kellerman thinks the soundtrack was "a little too on the nose," whatever that means. The new taco place by the old mall: Jonesy says the fried avocado taco is "to die for" and Kellerman says he doesn't eat green things.

This concerns Jonesy. "Nothing green? Broccoli? Salad?"

Kellerman shakes his head and shrugs. "I know, I know. I just . . . can't. But I take all kinds of supplements, so . . ."

I'm not convinced. "What about green apple Laffy Taffy?"

He laughs. "Doesn't count. I loooove green candy."

Jonesy looks appalled. "You're like a big kid!"

Mr. Kellerman laughs and shrugs again, and we all sit in comfortable silence for a bit before he speaks again. "Now all I can think about is Laffy Taffy."

Even Jonesy agrees. "It does sound really good."

Maybe ten minutes later, we head back to class. I dread opening that class door with every step. *Embarrassed* doesn't begin to cover it. I feel like a sideshow attraction being led in on a leash.

As expected, everyone turns when we walk in, and Elizabeth is the first one to say something. (She may be kind of annoying and up the teachers' butts, but she's genuinely nice.)

"Are you okay, Andrew?"

I give my best attempt at a smile and sit down at my table. "I'm okay. I . . . I guess I had a panic attack. So . . . yeah." I could do without everyone staring, but I figure it's best to call it what it was.

"Sorry, man. My mom gets those." It's Brady—one of the last kids I expected to be sympathetic.

"So does my older brother."

"That was wicked intense."

"I thought you were gonna die."

There are a lot of responses, all at once, so I don't catch all of them. Surprisingly, most of my classmates seem pretty understanding. I will say that Carly Gifford blurts out "You hit a teacher!" in an accusing way, but I hear Brady tell her to "be cool, Carly!" And Bobby Adams just sits and stares at me with his mouth slightly open—but Bobby's kind of a mouth-open starer on a good day, so I let it go.

Nurse Finnegan heads out, and I drop into my chair, exhausted. Not just exhausted. Wiped out. On empty. Drained.

Kellerman spends the last five minutes of the class talking with us about our upcoming art project, and I'm relieved to just zone out and listen. We'll each make a flying craft/object/thing out of clay, and then we'll have a contest to see whose flings the farthest across the room off of a big metal T square mounted to his desk. (He does this each year with the seventh grade and it's legendary. It's so Mr. Kellerman.)

I plan on making a squirrel in an aviator cap sitting on a toilet-plane.

Jonesy's making a hammerhead shark. Of course.

When the bell rings, the class heads out. A few people pat me on the back or ask if I'm okay, and Jonesy comes up and gives me a big bear hug. Then she holds me at arm's length.

"I have gym. I gotta go change. You okay, ding-dong?"

I nod and thank her and she heads out.

I head for the door, but when I get there, I turn and look back at Mr. Kellerman. He's kicked back behind his desk, watching me.

I'm not sure what to say, so I stick with the classics.

"Thank you. And I'm so sorry that I . . ." I can't even bring myself to say it again, but I think it:

I hit you. My favorite teacher by a mile. I hit you.

He smiles, twirls the end of his mustache—his signature move—and waves a hand at me like it was nothing. "Anytime, Andrew." Then he grabs a can of Diet Coke from the cooler behind his desk and cracks it open. "You're gonna be fine. And if you ever need to talk . . ."

I tap the doorframe five times, just because I feel like I should. "You bet."

But then I just stand there. Staring at the floor. Every ounce of energy has flooded out of me. I feel like a husk. Like a shell.

I look up at Kellerman, and he must see it in my eyes. He gets up and starts walking to me.

"Come on. Panic attacks'll wipe you out big time. Let's go see Gracie and you can just chill out."

I look at the empty room. "You don't have a class?"

"Nope."

We turn and start walking down the hall together. He's easy to be around. About halfway to the nurse's office, I ask him:

"Did you call Nurse Finnegan 'Gracie'?"

He smiles and strolls on. "I was kind of hoping you didn't catch that."

AFTER A PANIC ATTACK
FEEL LIKE A NOODLE!
I'M COOKED.
BRAIN DEAD!
CIRCUITS FRIED! (FRENCH FRIED!)
GET 'EM WHILE THEY'RE HOT!
ZZZZZ!
Z
Z

19

BACK AGAIN

When we walk into the nurse's office (again!) Kellerman announces our arrival.

"Gracie, I've brought you the Yaeger child. He's basically toast."

Nurse Finnegan turns and gives him a questioning look. "*Gracie*, Mr. Kellerman?"

He covers his face with one big hand, tragically. "I'm afraid the jig is up, dear. He's onto us."

Nurse Grace Finnegan puts her hands on her hips. "Well. We're just gonna have to kill him now. Leave no witnesses." Then she points at the couch. I roll my eyes and sit, flopping back against the wall.

"Just be cool about it. We don't need it on the evening news or anything."

My eyes are closed, so I just give a weak thumbs-up and a head nod. Teacher romance isn't all that interesting, if I'm honest.

"Coca-Cola?" Nurse F asks, and when I open my eyes, she's reaching into a mini-fridge in the corner. "It's my private stash."

"Yes. Thank you." It sounds amazing. "But I thought the Cheetos were your private stash."

Kellerman reels like he's taken a blow. "Wait. The kid knows about the Cheetos too? We're done for!"

I laugh, and just then Principal Espinosa half slides into the room. He sees me on the couch, being handed the Coke.

"Andrew! I was so hoping you had found your way here! I heard you had an unfortunate attack, dear boy." He actually said "dear boy," like we were in the 1800s or something. But the look of concern on his face is sincere. "Do you feel okay now? It seems you've had a day for the ages." He's still near the doorway as a student sprints past behind him and the bell rings.

"I'm okay. I'm just super tired. And worried. And kind of . . . done, I guess. Brain-dead."

"Understandable. I can only imagine the state you must be in. Please let me know if there's anything at all we can do." Then he leans against the doorjamb and looks tired. Finally, he looks up at Nurse Finnegan. "Do you happen to have any more of those Flamin' Hot Cheetos?"

Mr. Kellerman's hands shoot up in mock outrage. "ESPINOSA KNOWS ABOUT THE CHEETOS?? This thing goes all the way to the top!"

AUTHOR'S NOTE:

THIS BOOK IS NOT SPONSORED BY CHEETOS, ALTHOUGH THAT WOULD BE AWESOME.

Cheetos are distributed to all. As Nurse F hands me mine, I have to wonder: "A Coke and Flamin' Hot Cheetos? Is this approved treatment?"

"On my watch it is. Just don't tell the school board." She glances over at Principal Espinosa.

His eyebrows shoot up and he puts his hand on his chest like he's taking an oath. "I saw nothing."

I tear my bag open. I'm popping one in my mouth as I see a flash of bright pink go by in the hall behind my principal.

I freeze, and the Cheeto falls silently from my mouth.

"Wait. . . ."

Mr. Espinosa sees the look on my face. He stops chewing and asks if I'm okay.

"Was that my grandma?"

"Where??" For some reason, he looks down into his little bag.

"IN THE HALL!"

I fly off of the couch. It takes everyone a second to react, so I'm barging past Mr. Espinosa as he turns. I clear him and look down the hall and there she is.

Her neon-pink robe. A pretty bad case of bed head—one side is all smashed down. The fuzzy green Yoda slippers I gave her two years ago that I got on sale at CVS. She's shuffling away from us, but there's no mistaking her.

"G!!!" Somehow, the one syllable gets past the dump-truck-sized lump in my throat. My feet are frozen for some reason. Like, they can't believe she's here. At the school!

Mr. Espinosa calls out too. "Mrs. Hanley?"

G stops as Mr. Kellerman and Nurse Finnegan come into the hall behind me. After a second, she turns her head to look back. Then she slowly shifts her feet so she's facing us. She's looking straight at the principal.

"Mr. Espinosa, shouldn't you be in class?"

That breaks the spell. I run to put my arms around her—tears stinging my eyes. "You're okay! You're here!" She seems surprised but allows the hug. I mean, I guess she thinks she's back here teaching again?

Mr. Espinosa is smiling. "I'm actually the principal here now, Mrs. Hanley. If you can believe that."

G scoffs. "Pssh. And I'm the Queen of England. All I know is you'd better have a hall pass, Carlos."

This gets a chuckle from Mr. Kellerman.

Mr. Espinosa—Carlos??—comes up and gently puts a hand on her shoulder. "Your grandson and I—all of us—we've all been *terribly* worried, Mrs. H. Are you okay?"

That's when I see she's holding about a third of a chocolate glazed donut. So, she DID go to the Donut Den! She takes a bite and looks down at me. A few crumbs fly out when she speaks.

"Oh. Hey, Andrew."

20

OFFICE SPACE

Mrs. Dithers - Admin. Assistant

It's maybe fourteen minutes later, and we're in Principal Espinosa's office because there's more room in here than in the cramped nurse's office—and more people are on the way.

My mom and Mika have been called. They were beyond relieved and are getting here as fast as they can. G and I are in the two chairs in front of the desk.

She hasn't said much since we got in here—she's mostly been staring out the window, sipping from a cold bottle of water that Mrs. Dithers (nervously) brought her, and not answering our flurry of questions.

But she's smiling, and there are no signs that she's injured in any way—Nurse F has looked her over.

I could watch her sit there all day, just knowing she's okay.

I mean, I could also sleep for seventy thousand hours—the relief has made me even more drained, somehow—but I'll settle for watching G sip from her bottle.

Jonesy was called to the office too. She's lying on her back on a bench, kicking her feet and holding a basketball that she found here in the office. I think it'd been confiscated from a student. Somebody wrote *BANANA BUTT* on it, for some reason.

Mr. Espinosa is leaned way back in his chair, his tie loosened, looking very un-principal-like and almost as tired as I feel.

Suddenly, the office buzzer goes off and Mrs. Dithers lets my mom and Mika in. They arrive in a blubbery, excited tornado of relief and weepy apologies and hugs and more hugs. It's Hug-a-Palooza for a few minutes. Everybody gets one. Or two.

G, confused, gets the works.

WELCOME TO HUG-A-PALOOZA!!

It's only after my third lung-collapsing hug that my mom steps back and covers her mouth. Looks me up and down, taking it all in: the black eye, the stained face and shirt, the broken lens in my glasses.

"Andrew. My God! What on earth?" Her eyes are wide. "Your eye!" She gently touches the skin under my shiner.

I give her a weak, crooked smile. "It's . . . been a day."

This gets a blurt laugh from Jonesy. "He's not lying."

I'm worried about my mom. "What about your job? Is your boss going to fire you for leaving?"

"What? Oh!" My mom comes in for one more hug. "Not at all. Mr. McAndrews was wonderful! I was so rattled, he actually insisted on driving me home. And he helped us search for G!" Then in a slightly quieter voice: "His dad had Alzheimer's as well."

"Oh, that's really cool!" I hear it coming out of my mouth. "About him being nice, I mean. Not about . . . y'know . . . his dad having Alzheimer's."

Mika, on the bench by her daughter, laughs. "We knew what you meant, dingus."

Just then, the two police officers are let in as well. They look almost as relieved as my mom and Mika to see G sitting there in one piece. After checking her over, the male officer walks over and pats my back.

"You look like you could use a day at the spa, kid."

His partner Martinez makes a face. "The *spa*? Seriously, Davis?"

He hikes up his giant utility belt. "Whatever, Martinez." He looks around the room for support. "I keep telling her to try a pedicure. It's like a little slice of heaven for your feet, y'know?" He sees Mr. Kellerman in the corner and hooks a thumb at him. "This guy knows what I'm talkin' about, don't you?"

Kellerman just twirls his mustache and chuckles.

"You okay, ma'am?" Officer Davis places his hand on G's back. Her only response is a kind smile up at him.

"I've looked her up and down and she seems fine." Nurse F catches my mom's eye. "But she should see her doctor, obviously."

My mom just walks over and gives G another quiet hug, petting her hair.

Officer Davis is looking at me now. "And seriously, son. There *has* to be a story. What happened to you?"

Jonesy pipes up. "Gene Phillips happened to him, that's what."

Officer Davis's eyebrows shoot up as he looks over at the principal.

"Carl Phillips's kid? The construction guy?"

Mr. Espinosa nods and the two police officers exchange a knowing look. Officer Davis goes on. "Yeah, we know that kid. Been out to his house more times than I can count."

Well, *that* gets my interest. "Why? What'd he do?"

He shakes his head and grimaces. "Not for the kid." Officer Martinez shoots him a look that would shut *me* up.

"Never mind. I shouldn't have said anything."

Okay, that was weird. Huh.

That's when the intercom crackles to life. I hear Mrs. Dithers's voice both through the office door and over the speaker.

"It looks like we only have two homerooms left for photos! So, if Mr. Washington's and Ms. Evans's homeroom classes can be excused and proceed to the annex, that will be our last group. Thank you for your cooperation today!"

I laugh, and everyone in the office turns.

My mom is still looking me over. “What’s so funny?”

“That’s me. And Jonesy. Ms. Evans is homeroom teacher.” I give a tired smile and feel my swollen eye crinkle.

“It’s picture time!”

21

PICTURE TIME

Mr. Espinosa leans forward.

"Obviously, Andrew . . . Given your . . . current state—we can make other arrangements. Or you can just sit photos out this—"

I cut him off. "No, it's okay." I stand up slowly, using what feels like the very last ounce of energy in me. "I earned this photo."

Mr. Kellerman laughs. "Heck, yes."

I start for the door, and my mom puts her hand on my shoulder. "Andrew. You don't need to."

I turn and give her another hug. "I do, Mom. I'm fine." I think for a second. "Okay, not fine, but I'm fine."

I turn, and Jonesy and I head out the door. Mrs. Dithers watches as we pass her desk, and then we're in the hall.

A few other kids from our homeroom are heading to the Annex Room as well. Danny the Juice-Sprayer comes out of the band room as we pass.

"Andrew! Lookin' good, mate!"

Jonesy laughs and I give Danny a thumbs-up as he falls in beside us. I feel like a zombie, but maybe a relieved zombie?

I just keep repeating it in my head: G is okay. She's okay.

But it's more than that.

My kernel popped today. It exploded. It was the worst thing in the world that I could imagine, and I survived.

It was terrifying and epically embarrassing and basically a nightmare.

It was every bit as bad as I'd imagined—maybe worse—but I came out the other side.

I lived.

Barely.

My coping stuff from Dr. Cain helped. The breathing helped. Mr. K and Nurse F helped and Jonesy helped and . . . I helped *myself.* I remind myself again that there's a lot more to me than my anxiety.

As I walk down the hall next to my best friend and Danny the Juice King, I'm thinking: If I can survive that, I can survive anything.

We get to the darkened Annex Room behind a bunch of other students. When I step in, there's already a line, almost to the door. Jeri Hannum, at the back of the line, turns and sees it's me.

"Hey, Andrew." She smiles, and it seems like a genuinely caring smile. "Heard you're having a lousy day.

You all right?" A flash goes off at the front of the line. Then another.

"I'm doing better."

Tyler of the stew is in front of her. "Wow. That black eye just keeps getting uglier, doesn't it."

"Thanks, Tyler."

He looks like he feels bad for saying it. "I mean, you make it look . . ." His face drops. "Ah, crud."

He's looking past me, out the door. I turn to see what he's looking at.

It's Gene. Strolling down the hall like he owns the place. Unfortunately, he shares our homeroom, and here he comes in all his glory.

I feel Jonesy's hand on my arm.

I expect the anxiety. The tightening of the shoulders, the heating up of my already popped kernel.

But it doesn't come.

Maybe my body, my brain, my system . . . maybe they're too wiped out. Maybe all my "freak-out circuits" are fried. When I see Gene coming, all I feel is exhausted, really. Like, tired in the bones.

Gene steps through the doorway, and as his eyes adjust to the darkened room, I step up to him.

"Hey, Gene."

Gene looks surprised that I'm approaching him—and calmly too.

He puts on his official Gene the Mean smirk. "Green Shoes."

I rub the back of my neck. "Can we talk? Like, just talk for a second?"

He sneers. "Get bent, Garage Sale."

I continue. "No, I'm serious."

I'm honestly not sure what's gotten into me. Do I really think I can reason with Gene now? I glance behind me and realize we have an audience. At least the next five or six kids in front of me in line have all turned around. Jonesy has a worried look on her face. I turn back as another camera flash goes off.

"Gene, do you remember when you invited me to your birthday party? In third grade? The one where your dad got the Marvel characters in costume?"

"I told you, I don't want to talk to you. So, shut up or I'll shut you up."

I sigh. "I hear you. But listen. You did, actually. Invite me. And it was a great party."

Gene cracks his neck. "You are such a dork. We literally invited most of the school, so what's your point?"

Behind me, I hear Tyler whine, "I didn't get invited." Someone shushes him.

"I'm not sure I really have a point, Gene, I'm just . . ."

"Yeager. Stop. Or I promise you will eat your teeth."

I turn around and see Jonesy and several other students watching. I must be delirious, because it urges me to go on.

"Can't we be more mature than this?"

Apparently, I'm getting into it, because—in grand G fashion—I throw my arms out wide like I'm—completely unlike myself—about to go on a heroic rant to Gene about how we all have to get along, and Peace and Love and blah blah blah, but what happens is I feel my hand connect with something.

It connects hard.

POP!

I turn around fast enough that I see Gene's look of surprise. His arm is cocked back—he was stepping in, ready to do some Gene-Punching, but my wide-flailing arm has nailed him—perfectly—on the nose.

I'm as shocked as he is. His eyes slam shut and he

just . . . crumples. It's like all the strength goes out of his legs and he goes down like a Jenga tower. He lands on his butt and his hands go to his nose.

"YOU SHARK BOPPED HIM!" Jonesy sounds overcome with joy. "He was coming for you and you SHARK BOPPED HIM!"

"Everything okay back there?" It's the photographer. He can't see us around the reflective shade thing. "Somebody bopped what?"

Jonesy calls back to him, "Everything's fine!" Then she actually laughs. Somebody behind me says, "So rad!"

I'm in shock. "NO! No, Gene! I didn't . . . You know me! I hate violence!" I step over and reach a hand out to him. "Violence is never the answer! That's my motto! I'm a peaceful . . ."

Gene swats my hand away and opens his eyes. They're

full of tears from the hit to the nose. "Stop, Yaeger. Just stop." Then his eyes squint up again. "Aw, man. Gawd, that hurts."

I take a step back. "I really didn't do that on purpose." Jonesy and Tyler are patting me on the back like I won a prize fight. "Gene, I was just gesturing—I talk with my hands—and . . ."

"Yaeger. Seriously, shut up." Gene wipes under his nose and checks his hand for blood. When he sees there isn't any, he runs it through his hair. He hawks and spits on the floor next to him—gross—and puts his head in his hands.

"Are . . . are you okay?" I have no idea how to react.

I feel a couple other hands pat me on the back.

The photographer keeps taking photos behind me, and I really don't know what to say. Finally—slowly—Gene stands up. I take two steps back, but all he does is glare at me. At the others standing around.

"This is stupid. I don't want a stupid school picture anyway."

Gene straightens his shirt and heads for the door. He's maybe ten feet away when I speak up.

"I still have a photo. From that day. It's you and me with the Iron Man guy."

Gene stops, but he's still facing away.

I go on. "I mean, it's on a board with a bunch of photos, so your . . . your face is kind of covered up, but it's still there."

Gene, still facing away, lowers his head.

"None of us want to fight with you, Gene. You used to be kind of . . . fun."

He stands there for a few seconds while the flash pops a couple more times. When he speaks, it's so low I can barely hear it.

"I heard they found your grandma. I'm glad she's not dead or anything."

"Thanks."

Then he turns around to look me in the eyes, and he's all Gene again. "But if you ever call me Eugene again, I'll put your face through a brick wall."

I nod a couple times. "Fair enough."

Gene walks away then, but just as he's framed in the

door—silhouetted by the light of the hall—the intercom squawks, and out comes Mrs. Dithers's voice.

"Gene Phillips, please report to the office. Thank you."

Gene comes to a stop for a split second before his head drops and he turns the corner.

I turn back and several kids' mouths are hanging open at what just went down.

Jonesy is beaming. "Shark bops work, am I right?"

Just then, I get a whiff of something horrible. Jonesy pulls her jersey up over her nose. "Oh, what in the . . . ?"

"Tyler!!" I know that smell.

Tyler is backing away. "Sorry! Tiny stew burp! Take it up with my mom!"

Jonesy and I move ten feet away, by the wall. I can tell by her eyes that she's smiling under her shirt-mask.

"What? I thought you were mad at me? I thought I was a huge jerk."

Now she shrugs. "Well . . . yeah. You *were* kind of a jerk."

I give her a tired, sad smile. "I was. Jonesy, I'm really sorry. I'll be better. Okay? You have my word."

She bobs her head around a little like she's considering, then bumps my shoulder with hers. "All right." Then she looks deadly serious. "But I'm holding you to it. I'm watching." She squints and points two fingers at her eyes, then at mine.

This makes me laugh. "And I was thinking. We should absolutely sit with your team tomorrow, y'know?"

She lowers her shirt and smiles. "That sounds good. They're super nice, I swear." Then she breaks into a big wide grin again.

"What?"

She laughs. "You are going to have the most epic yearbook photo ever. This thing may go viral."

I smile, even though it crinkles my busted eye. "Right?"

"Seriously. Wear it proud."

"Oh, I'm gonna." I *am* kind of low-level excited to see how bad it comes out. We stand in silence and watch Tyler and Jeri get photographed. Then Danny gets called, and we'll be next.

Jonesy leans in. "That was pretty amazing with Gene back there. Andrew Yaeger: Gene Whisperer. It actually kind of inspired me."

"How so?"

She grins super wide. "Eh. I'm gonna talk to my dad myself. I appreciate your offer to do it, but . . . it should be me. I'll let him know I just want to play for the team. Maybe a few games on the side, but I'm not looking to be the WNBA's first round draft pick anytime soon."

"He'll be fine. Seriously. Your dad is one of the good ones. He's just been doing what he thought you—"

The photographer takes his last photo of Danny, turns, and calls out. "Next!"

Jonesy smiles and pushes me forward. I step into the well-lit area.

The photographer sees me, and his face drops. He looks me up and down—the whole glorious mess.

I pull my shoulders back. "You know what? I've never been more sure of anything. Let's do this."

He nods his head, then chuckles and steps out of the way. "Well, if you say so. Step right up. Hop on that stool."

I do. After giving him my name and confirming the spelling, he heads behind the camera. He gets a good look at me through the lens and pokes his head back up.

"You're *sure*?"

"Absolutely."

"You, um . . . you want a comb?"

"Nope. As is." This gets a laugh from the photographer and some of the students.

He makes some final adjustments. "Well, this is one for the books."

You have no idea, I think.

Then I throw my shoulders back and give the biggest, goofiest grin I can manage without my face hurting too bad.

I take a deep breath.

And then another.

And then the camera clicks.

Yaeger, Andrew

AUTHOR'S NOTE

I didn't write about anxiety by accident. It's part of me. I was 100 percent a "Kid with Anxiety."

I've dealt with it for as long as I can remember. Situational anxiety, but also that free-floating kind that gets after you for no reason and feels like a head full of bees. I had it bad . . . and as a kid I didn't even know what to call it.

I thought everybody worried themselves sick all day long. I thought everyone had that "bad electricity" running through them, and lay in bed at night, overwhelmed and stressing about pretty much everything their brain could get its hands on.

I had it bad enough that I actually used to be sick—almost every day—before school. Grade school, middle school, high school. I had gut problems, nausea, and worse. I'd be doubled over in pain, watching kids walk by on their way to school, hoping it would clear soon enough that I wouldn't be late and need a note. It was awful. For years my doctors thought I was lactose intolerant.

Nope. Turns out I was Stress Intolerant.

I learned early on that anxiety can absolutely drain you—like a parked car with its lights on. It just sucks the life force out of you. I'd come home exhausted by my own thoughts. Some of that was from the OCD, which came along in middle school.

Tapping things, arranging things, checking and rechecking door locks and flipping light switches X number of times.

I also learned the hard way that being wiped out like that can lead to depression. I've dealt with it on and off for most of my life, and it's very much intertwined with the anxiety.

I've learned to handle these things better now, but they don't really go away. You just learn how to tell them to be quiet. And sometimes—most times, maybe—that works.

But so many of you have kindly helped to kick obstacles out of my way—especially the ones I put there myself. I'm still learning how to tell that voice in my head to kick rocks when I need it to.

And I'm getting better at it.

SPECIAL THANKS

I have a million people to thank for helping me get this book written. An enormous bear hug of thanks to my superhero of an editor, Kate Harrison, for helping me see the things I can't and making sure all the angles were covered. The same giant heartfelt thanks to Dan Lazar, super agent and part-time guidance counselor. These two are the dream team every writer hopes for. And all of you at Dial Books for Young Readers—Michelle Lee, Olivia Russo, plus Jason Henry and Maya Tatsukawa for your incredible design work—you are amazing. Thank you thank you thank you to the entire Penguin team. Also a huge thank-you to Torie Doherty Munro, Cecilia de la Campa, and Alessandra Birch at Writer's House.

As always, *enormous* thanks to my amazing family and friends for their insane feats of patience. Writing a book can be a long, messy, anxiety-inducing process, and for any tiny amount of that stuff that spilled onto you, I apologize.

I'd like to say a special thanks to Polly Larson for her incredibly helpful advice and insight when it came to how kids—and therapists—deal with these complicated issues these days. Polly, you're the best. Also, to my own doctors and therapists over the years who have gotten me this far—it hasn't always been pretty, but here we are.

I'd also like to thank my friends Larry Mitchell and Bill Chlystun, who opened up about their own families' very personal experiences with Alzheimer's. I know from them that everyone's experience with this disease is unique, and I can only hope I've done them justice.

Thank you so much, Jeff Winston (aka Cuz), for helping me when I completely forgot how to diagram a sentence. (It's been a while!) Teachers for the win!

Finally, thank you to everyone who has ever sat with me on a step, a curbside, a bench, held my hand, or taken a long walk with me to tell me everything will be okay. Friends, loved ones, teachers, mentors. All of you. Thank you all for rubbing my back, giving me a much-needed hug, and assuring me that the world was not, in fact, ending.

Thank you all so, so much.

—Rob

Humiliating Author Photo

FURTHER READING AND OTHER COOL STUFF

ANXIETY AND OCD RESOURCES

Books

- *The Worry (Less) Book: Feel Strong, Find Calm and Tame Your Anxiety!* by Rachel Brian. Wren & Rook.

- *My Anxious Mind: A Teen's Guide to Managing Anxiety and Panic* by M. A. Tompkins and K Martinez. Magination Press.

- *What to Do When Your Brain Gets Stuck: A Kid's Guide to Overcoming OCD* by D. Huebner. Magination Press.

Websites

- Anxiety UK at anxietyuk.org.uk

- Young Minds at youngminds.org.uk

ALZHEIMER'S RESOURCES

Books

- *Grandma and Me: A Kid's Guide for Alzheimer's & Dementia* by Beatrice Tauber Prior Psy.D. and Mary Ann Drummond RN. Morgan James Publisher.

- *Meet Me Where I Am: An Alzheimer's Care Guide* by Mary Ann Drummond. Morgan James Publisher.

- *The 36-Hour Day: A Family Guide to Caring for People Who Have Alzheimer Disease and Other Dementias* by Nancy L. Mace and Peter V. Rabins. Johns Hopkins University Press.

Website

- Alzheimer's Society at alzheimers.org.uk

BY THE SAME AUTHOR

One of the 10 Best YA and Children's Books of 2020
– *TIME* magazine